Stay Tuned for Terror

Look for these SpineChillers™ Mysteries

Stay Tuned for Terror

Fred E. Katz

Thomas Nelson, Inc.

Nashville

Published in Nashville, Tennessee, by Tommy Nelson™, a division of Thomas Nelson, Inc. SpineChillers™ Mysteries is a trademark of Thomas Nelson, Inc.

Scripture quoted from the *International Children's Bible, New Century Version,* copyright © 1983, 1986, 1988 by Word Publishing. Used by permission.

Storyline: Tim Ayers

Library of Congress Cataloging-in-Publication Data
Katz, Fred E.
    Stay tuned for terror / Fred E. Katz.
       p. cm. — (SpineChillers mysteries ; 10)
    Summary: Twelve-year-old Bethany and her friends need to call on God for courage when their audition for the local television show "Tales of Terror" brings them in contact with some scary creatures.
    ISBN 0-8499-4053-2
    [1. Horror Stories   2. Christian life—Fiction.]   I. Title.
II. Series: Katz, Fred E. SpineChillers mysteries ; 10.
PZ7.K1573St 1997
[Fic]—dc21
   97-11090

                            CIP
                            AC

Printed in the United States of America

97 98 99 00 01 02 QKP 9 8 7 6 5 4 3 2 1

"Which way do I go now? Every tree looks exactly alike, and the sun is going down. I'm lost. Absolutely lost," the boy moaned as he stood looking up at the tall dark trees. The sun sank behind the hill. Bats swooped through the treetops.

The boy ran and dodged the thorny bushes as best he could. But they kept scratching and cutting at his legs. Blood dripped from his knees and into his muddy socks. As the night grew blacker and blacker, fear grew in his mind and heart.

"Which way?" he cried again. But there is no one to hear him. The boy fell to the ground. "I can't go another step. Maybe I should just sleep now and look for a way back to camp in the morning. That's a good idea. . . . But what about the monster that's supposed to roam the woods around Camp YelloJello?

"Why did I leave camp by myself? What a stupid idea. A kid could get killed out here, or even worse. If I get back, I'll never do anything like this again." He sat quietly and tried to calm his fears.

"Why did I keep asking the counselors to tell me so many monster stories?" he wondered aloud. "All I can think about is those stories. I'm scared. I'm hungry. I'm lost. Remembering those stories makes it all worse."

He got up and wandered through the woods talking to himself. "One counselor told me that a monster comes out of the woods at night, looking for stray campers. It's half bear and half man. He snatches kids up and carries them back to his hiding place for a feast of camper stew. Every year Camp YelloJello loses a camper. No one has been taken this summer, but the counselor reminded me that the summer is only half over. Now, it looks like I'll be the first."

While he walked, he looked for any signs of a pathway or even a place to hide and sleep. In the darkness it was hard to see. With each step, the boy's fear grew. His hands felt cold and clammy. He kept wiping them on his shorts, but it didn't help much.

Suddenly his nose caught the smell of a camp fire. Breaking into a grin, he thought aloud, "I must be close to Camp YelloJello. Great! My friends are going to be glad to see me. I've been gone so long. But what am I going to tell the camp director? . . . I don't want to say anything to anybody. I just want to get back and have some dinner."

The camper laughed to himself. "Even camp food

sounds good. I can't wait to sit down at one of those cold, wooden tables and stick my fork into mystery meat. The last time I had it, I could have thrown it across the room like a Frisbee. When I suggested it, my counselor wasn't too impressed, but the other kids thought it was cool. This time I'll eat everything put in front of me, even if it can fly."

As the boy nearly ran to the top of the hill, he could see sparks flying in the air from the fire. It blazed higher than any he'd ever seen before at Camp YelloJello. "Maybe the counselor built it so big so I could find my way back to them," he mused.

At the top of the hill, the lost camper could see the whole fire. No one was near it. He decided everyone must be out looking for him. He headed down the hill toward the flames. As he got closer, he heard a strange ripping and tearing sound. The camper hesitated for a moment, then started to move cautiously toward the fire. When he came to a large tree, he stopped and stood behind it, listening carefully. He wanted to see what had made the tearing noise, but he didn't want to be seen.

He heard it again. The boy looked all around, but nothing was there. Then he heard something that sounded like very large feet walking. Twigs crackled and popped. Across from the boy, something came out of the woods. It was huge like a bear, but it had the face of a man. The face was twisted in a joyful smile as the creature ripped apart what he held and shoved bits of it into his mouth.

The camper took a step back. A tree limb stuck him in the ribs, and he yelped. The monster looked up. Their eyes connected. The monster snarled out, "Ah, dessert."

"*Tales of Terror* will be right back after these words from your local sponsor," the TV host said. The four of us were so engrossed in the TV movie that we groaned when the commercial came on.

"I hate that. I hate when they cut it off at the scariest moment just for a commercial," Kari complained.

"This is one of the best programs on. Where else could you get so scared by a place called Camp YelloJello?" I asked. My three friends agreed with me. Kari Roland had just moved to our neighborhood from some city in Mississippi. It wasn't one of the really big ones, so I can never remember the name of it.

Juan Angulo moved to our small city before my family did. He was born in Mexico, lived in Texas, and then came here before he was even old enough to start school. I should say that *here* is called Grove City, Florida. It isn't a big town, but it isn't too small either.

Matthew Stock was born in Grove City. His father

was also born in Grove City. So was his grandfather. They had both been mayor of the town. I guess Matthew is destined to be the mayor too. He plans to stay in Grove City all of his life.

I'm Bethany Blue. My family moved here because of my mom's job. At twelve, I'm the oldest of four kids in my family. My brother Peter is two years younger. My sisters, Rachel and Ruthie, are six and four. They're good kids, except when Peter messes with my stuff. That is one thing I don't like.

My friends and I were watching our favorite show, *Tales of Terror.* It runs horror movies, and it is hosted by four kids our age.

"I wish we could be the hosts of *Tales of Terror.* We could do a better job than those kids do," I said as we sat through a car commercial.

Juan pretended he was one of the hosts. "And now, little kiddies, brace yourselves for terror. Don't turn around. Don't move. We are right there with you. Ha, ha, ha."

Matthew grinned and said that he was going to get something to eat while the commercial was on. He only took one step before Juan yelled, "Look at the TV!" Matthew spun around. A man who said he was *Tales of Terror's* executive producer was on the screen.

He explained, "Our four hosts have been with us a long time. We appreciate what they've done in making *Tales of Terror* the number one show on our station. But they all want to move on to other projects. WTNP is looking for another group of kids to become our new hosts.

"If you and your friends are twelve years old or older, we invite you to audition. All you have to do is write a 500-word essay telling us why you want to be the hosts. If your essay is chosen, we will ask you to audition live in our studios. So grab your pens and send your essay to the address on your screen."

We looked at each other with our mouths wide open. We couldn't believe it. Maybe *we* could host the show from those spooky sets. This was the chance of a lifetime.

"Let's do it!" Matthew yelled.

"What are we going to write? It has to be a killer of an essay if we want to win the chance for a screen test," Kari stated.

"I don't think it would be hard. We've all got great imaginations, and Juan is the school's best English student," I encouraged.

Juan shook off fake applause as a display of his humility. We all laughed until we were distracted by the *Tales of Terror* hosts coming back on the TV. "Wow, what an ending! I think that was the scariest show ever. See you next week."

"We missed the end! I can't believe we missed it!" Matthew shrieked in mock pain. "Now, we'll have to wait until the reruns before we can see how it ended."

Juan walked up to Matthew, put his arm around him, and said, "No, we won't. If we're the new hosts, then I'm sure we can borrow a video or two."

I smiled at that thought. It would really be great to be on TV. I wondered if any of my other friends would treat me differently when I was a big TV star. I promised myself that I would give them all autographs whenever they asked.

I broke out of my daydreaming, looked at the others, and asked, "What are we going to write to get on that show? Any suggestions? I think I have some good ideas." The other three gathered close.

Each day after we sent in the essay, I ran to the mailbox the moment I got home from school. I wanted to see if we had been selected for an interview. By the end of the second week, I had lost hope. I was getting ready to call the other three and tell them that we may as well give up, when the phone rang. I leaped off my bed and grabbed it before the second ring.

"Hello, Blue residence. May I help you?" I chirped into the phone.

"Yes, this is Chuck Christensen, the producer for *Tales of Terror*," the voice said through the line. "May I speak with Bethany Blue, please?"

We must have won a screen test! I was cheering inside, but I needed to stay calm so I could get all the information from Mr. Christensen.

"This is me, I mean she. Well, you know what I mean," I stammered nervously with my voice cracking on every high syllable.

"Congratulations, you and your three friends have

won an opportunity to test to be the hosts of the *Tales of Terror* TV show," he said. I thought his voice sounded very familiar.

"Excuse me, sir, but you sound just like the man who's on in the mornings. You know, that Sailor Sam guy," I boldly said.

"You think so, huh? Well, there's a good reason for it. I *am* Sailor Sam," he told me.

What a great day I was having. First we won a chance to audition for a TV show. And I heard the news from my favorite TV character from when I was a little kid.

We were nervous the day of our screen test. I barely slept the night before, and the other three told me they had trouble sleeping too. We'd all been up watching reruns of *Tales of Terror.* That didn't make it easy to fall asleep either.

Our parents had all agreed to let us walk together. They couldn't all get off work. But we each had to have one parent there. We'd arranged to meet them at the station. On the way there, Juan told us about his dream. He always had exciting adventures in his sleep. They were a lot of fun to listen to too.

In Juan's dream we were all sitting inside a large casket and hosting the show. We had colas to drink and corn chips to munch on as we watched the movie from a TV monitor mounted in the casket's top. The show was called "Kid Dracula." The star had moved to Smalltown from his home in Transylvania because his dad had gotten a job at the Smalltown blood bank.

Juan said, "The dream was really going great until Kid Dracula showed up. He slammed the lid down on our coffin and locked us all in. He planned to ship us back to his home in Transylvania where he would keep us as his personal blood bank."

Kari was always a little skeptical, and she asked, "So, how did we get out?"

"When the shipping clerks picked us up, one of them lost his grip. The casket went flying. When it landed, it burst open. Then I leaped to my feet and fought with Kid Dracula," he went on.

"Did you win?" I asked.

"Of course! It was my dream, wasn't it?" Juan answered while he laughed. Juan made the walk fun, and before we realized it, the four of us were standing in front of the television studio.

"This is it," Matthew said, more like it was an ending rather than a great beginning.

"Matthew, I think we'll put you in charge of the 'absolute obvious.' You seem to be pretty good at pointing it out to us all," Kari told him.

Kari was the practical one in our group of friends. She was the type of person who always wanted proof. A few weeks ago in our Sunday school class, she asked our teacher, Beth, to explain what Christians believe about the afterlife. Beth explained what Jesus said about heaven and hell. Then she added the apostle Paul's comments about "dying once and then the judgment."

Kari wasn't satisfied. She asked Beth, "So what are ghosts then? I've always thought ghosts were people who died but hadn't gone on to heaven yet."

Beth answered that Kari's question was a good one. Then she asked, "If we die and instantly go before God, then what does that leave to roam around the spirit dimension?"

Kari thought for a moment. "Angels and demons."

"Where does the ghost come from if it is doing wicked things?" Beth continued questioning.

"It must be a demon," Kari said. You could see the light bulb come on inside her head. "That all makes sense except . . . ," Kari continued.

"Except what?" Beth inquired.

"Except it seems like everything I read talks about ghosts. And TV shows have ghosts on them. People see ghosts all the time."

Beth smiled at her. "Kari, I want you to do some research. Find every place in the Bible that talks about ghosts. Then find all the references about demons. I think you will come up with your answer by doing that."

Kari is still working on her assignment. She is good for us all because she asks good questions. As Christians we need to be challenged to think about the details. It's good for the brain and for the soul.

I took the lead and walked toward the front door. My mom and the others' parents were there waiting for us. I expected the building to be a lot bigger, but our local TV station has a fairly small studio.

As we walked into the marble foyer of the building, a receptionist looked up from her desk and gave us a big smile. She greeted us by saying, "You must be the last group of kids. Mr. Christensen said that you would be here about now. He's asked that you wait in the studio down the hall. Go that way, turn to your left, and you'll see a door on the right. Wait there. After he talks to your parents, he will come to the studio." She turned to our parents and asked them to follow a teenage boy nearby. "Sam will escort you to Mr. Christensen's office."

After they left, the receptionist motioned us on toward the studio, and went back to answering her phones.

We headed down the hall. We were more quiet than we'd ever been before. I had a case of stage fright, and I was sure the others did as well. When we got to the end of the hall I turned right.

"Bethany, weren't we supposed to turn left?" Kari questioned. "Then the studio is on the right."

"I don't know. This place is kind of overwhelming. Does anyone else remember?" I asked.

Juan said, "We're okay. There's a door up there on the left. Sailor Sam ought to be along soon to take us on the good ship *Fright.*"

We pushed the door open. The room was very

14

dark. I noticed some chairs along the wall near the door when we walked in. The only light in the room came streaming through the open door. We felt our way to the seats and sat down.

"This is a little strange. Why do they have it so dark in the studio where they're doing our screen test? You'd think that they'd light us up so they could see my dashing good looks," Matthew joked.

"Maybe they heard about you and decided a dark room would be better," Juan shot back at Matthew, then grinned.

"Thanks!" Matthew retorted.

"Cut it out. We need to show them how well we get along and work together," I reminded the others.

"This is silly," Kari said. "I'm turning the light on." She felt around for a switch and flicked it. Our eyes had gotten accustomed to the dark. I slapped my hands over my face to protect them from the blinding light. In a moment I was able to open my eyes, but what I saw made me want to close them again.

Across the room was a coffin. The man inside it sat up quickly, stretching his arms toward us.

I screamed, and my scream was joined by Juan's and then Matthew's. Kari also screeched at the top of her lungs. The man inside the coffin leaped out of it and started toward us.

Kari hit the door first and went shooting out into the hall. Matthew and Juan raced out after her. I hesitated, frozen in my tracks. Unfortunately, the man from the coffin hadn't been frozen in his.

He grabbed me by the shoulder and spun me around. I was staring into the face of the most normal-looking person I had ever seen. I stammered out, "You're not a vampire."

"No, I'm just one of the cameramen. I was taking a nap between my shifts. The coffin is the most comfortable place around here to lie down. I'm really sorry I scared you kids. I guess if I saw a man leap out of a coffin in a dark room, I'd scream and run too. Why were you four in here?" the cameraman asked me.

I was starting to calm down as I answered, "We're here to do a screen test for *Tales of Terror.*"

"Great. I'm the cameraman for the test. My name is Rick Krauser. I hope you do well. I have a great time working on the show. Maybe we'll end up working together," he said with a friendly smile.

"I guess we found the wrong room. Could you tell me where the studio for our screen test is?" I asked.

"Just follow me. I should have been there a few minutes ago." He led me out of the room. The other three were standing in the hallway looking very embarrassed.

"This is Rick Krauser. He is going to be our cameraman on the screen test," I told them.

They nodded hello and followed us when I motioned with my hand. We ended up in the right studio. We were inside for only a moment when Chuck Christensen walked in.

"Hi, kids, I hope I haven't kept you waiting too long. It can get awfully boring just sitting around, can't it?" he said.

"We weren't bored," I answered him honestly.

"Good, then let's get started. The screen test is simple. You need to go through that door over there marked *Terror.* Once you do, you're on," Mr. Christensen said.

Kari stepped toward him, raised her hand, and

asked, "What are we supposed to do once we go through that door?"

"Just be yourselves. There is nothing special that you have to do. Just let the set do it all for you," he grinned a sinister little smile and motioned for us to go ahead. We followed his instructions and went into the next room.

The room was dark. In fact, it was pitch-black. When the door closed behind us, I could not see a thing. My first thought was about how Kari had flipped the switch on in the last room. I whispered, "Kari?"

"Don't worry. I'm not going to do it again," she responded as quickly as I asked. "But I would like to know what's going to happen next. I didn't appreciate the way that old Sailor Sammy grinned at us. Something is going to happen, and I'm not sure I'm going to like it."

Kari barely finished her words when I heard the sound of claws scratching on the hard floor. The sound got closer. I felt us all move closer to each other. I was glad that I ended up with someone on either side of me.

The scratching got nearer. We could hear breathing. We could feel the breath. It was hot, and it smelled like rotting meat.

"What do we do?" Matthew asked.

"Anyone for a brisk run around the room?" Juan

joked, but nobody laughed. It may have helped him relieve his tension, but it didn't work for the rest of us.

The breathing sounded and felt like some creature stood only inches from our faces. I took a step back, and so did the others. I tried to take another when I bumped into the wall. This screen test could end up being a scream test!

For the moment we stood silently. The breathing had stopped. We relaxed. Suddenly, a spotlight lit the ground right in front of us. Something big and hairy leaped toward us. The light glistened off its long, razor-sharp teeth. The beast's mouth was open, and it growled like a wolf.

"Arrr!"

We braced ourselves against the hungry werewolf. I closed my eyes and starting praying. I waited. We all waited. Nothing got us. Nothing at all.

I opened my eyes, but I couldn't see anything. The room was pitch-black again. I couldn't hear anything, or smell the hot breath. Our attacker left as quickly as it came.

"Wow," Kari said. "That was great! My heart's still pounding."

Matthew spoke up, "What happened? I was sure that we were going to be lunch."

Another light came on. The beam focused on a dark figure wearing a long black cape on the other side of the room. He held the cape stretched across his face with his forearm. It blocked our view of everything but the man's eyes. Even that little bit of a view sent a wave of fear from my brain down to my heart.

He dropped the cape from his face and spoke, "I

am sorry, children, if my little pet, Wolfie, scared you. He doesn't mean any harm. He's very friendly once he gets to know you."

"Are you who we think you are?" I asked.

"No, I'm not," he answered. "You think I'm an actor playing the part of Dracula."

"You look just like Dracula," Matthew told him.

The man in black looked us in the eyes as he strolled closer and spoke again, "As I said, you thought that I was an actor. . . ."

I heard Matthew gulp. If he wasn't an actor then he must be . . . no, that was impossible. Out of nowhere a thick puff of red smoke engulfed him as a dim light came on. Out of the smoke flew a bat.

As it sailed toward us, my friends and I dove to the floor. I rolled over to look at Dracula. He was gone. I jumped up, pointed to where he had been, and said, "Look, he's gone!"

"That's because I'm over here."

I twirled around and stood eye to eye with Dracula. My mouth fell open, and my eyes must have been as big as baseballs.

"Did my little trick scare you?" he asked. "Good!" He laughed a spooky laugh. "Since you like my magic so much, perhaps I should charge you for it."

He drummed his fingers on his chin as he thought. "What would be a fair price?"

Snapping his fingers, he said, "I've got it. I know

what the price of admission should be. How about a pint of blood from each of you?"

I screamed and ran across the room as fast as my legs could carry me. I looked back to see if Dracula was chasing me. He wasn't, but my three friends were gaining on me. I bumped into the wall and the other three slid into me.

Juan yelled, "Where is he?"

"I can't see him anywhere," Matthew answered.

"This scares me," said Kari. "What do we do next?"

"How do we get out of here? I don't think I like this place anymore," I said as I felt my stomach flip.

"Think we can get to the door before he appears again?" Juan whispered.

"Let's try!" Kari said.

The four of us fairly flew across the room toward the door. Matthew got there first. The door flew open, and Matthew leaped into the arms of Frankenstein. The rest of us stopped so fast our tennis shoes screeched.

Matthew screamed and kicked and screamed again. I looked at Kari and Juan in desperation. "We've got to do something to help him."

Frankenstein started to squeeze Matthew. Our friend looked as scared as anyone I had ever seen.

Juan grabbed a broom from beside the door and held it like a baseball bat. He started toward Frankenstein as he said, "Let go of my friend!"

Amazingly, Frankenstein took a step forward and dropped Matthew at Juan's feet. Then he took a step back, and the door swung closed.

We were safe!—at least for the moment. But before we could even catch our breath, I heard another door behind us open.

"Bravo, bravo," we heard a voice say. I jerked my body around and saw Mr. Christensen.

"That was excellent, kids. You had the greatest expressions on your faces. The screen test went very well. Let me introduce you to our ghosts, goblins, and ghouls here on *Tales of Terror*," he said as he moved his hand toward the door where Frankenstein stood. "Frankenstein was played by John Cross. You also see him as the weatherman on the evening news, without his makeup, of course. Dracula is Keith Krispin, our anchorman. The Wolfman is a video projection. We use a lot of those on our sets."

"I was pretty scared. We're going to have a fantastic time being around here every week. I can't wait for the fun to begin," Juan said.

"We really like what you did, but we do have another team of kids that we are considering. We'll let you know in a few days," Chuck said.

Kari asked, "Who are the others?"

"They're not from your school, but you may know them. They won the county science fair last year," he told us.

I got a sinking feeling inside. The other team was made up of four computer wizards. I hoped that their expertise in computers wouldn't overshadow our expertise in looking frightened to death.

"We'll call you in a few days for a second screen test. Right now, I've got to make sure that the news gets on at the right time. It was nice to meet all of you," Mr. Christensen said as he exited.

"It looks like we might be on TV," Matthew joyfully told us.

"Don't count your chickens before they're hatched," Kari warned him.

"That seems like a downer attitude," I said to her.

"It is. But we can't go running around saying that we're the hosts of *Tales of Terror* until we've signed on the dotted line," she responded. "So let's work on getting past the next screen test. I have a feeling it's going to be really scary."

Before we could plan how we'd prepare for the second screen test, we heard a loud cry from outside the door.

We raced into the hallway expecting to find a were-wolf or something running free. Our friend, Rick Krauser, was standing in the middle of the hall with his left hand wrapped around his right thumb.

He looked up from his thumb toward us and said, "Sorry, kids. I guess that's the second time I scared you today. I smashed my thumb in the door."

Juan said, "That's all right. We need to get used to being frightened in case we end up being the hosts of *Tales of Terror*. Is your thumb okay?"

"I'll be fine. I hope it all works out for you. Maybe I'll be seeing you around sometime. Maybe even sooner than you think."

His words made my curiosity sensor go off. I wondered what he meant.

My mom offered to drive us home, but we turned her down. We thought a nice walk would settle our nerves a bit. After everything we had been through, I was happy to face nothing more frightening than a calm stroll down the quiet streets of Grove City.

A few blocks from my house, I stopped the others in the middle of the sidewalk and said, "Do you realize that God answered our prayers? We prayed that we would have a chance to audition. Let's thank the Lord for what he's already done and ask for his help to do our best in the next audition."

In our youth group we had been learning about prayer. It seemed natural now for us to stand in a circle in public and pray. When we finished, I felt like God had control of what was going to happen.

Over the next few days, the most terrifying thing that I faced was the wait. Our friends who knew about the screen test were anxious to know who would be the new hosts of *Tales of Terror*. But none of them was as anxious as we were.

On Friday after our first screen test, the station still had not called. I raced home with Matthew alongside me. We both hoped we would hear that Mr. Christensen had called. I pushed the door open and yelled, "Mom, I'm home. Did I get any phone calls?" It was Mom's day to be home early.

No response. Mom usually lets me know right where she is. I called out again and still there wasn't any answer. I turned to Matthew and said, "I guess she went out. Whenever she does that she leaves me a note on the fridge."

Mom's note said she had gone to the store and would be back later. I looked near the phone to see if there were any messages. Nothing. I told Matthew,

"The television station must not have called." As I pointed toward the phone, it rang.

"That's freaky," Matthew said.

"Wow, it sure is. I hope it's the station." I picked up the receiver and said, "Hello."

A strange voice replied, "Hello, is Bethany Blue at home?"

"I'm Bethany."

"We're calling from the *Tales of Terror* show. We have narrowed our selection for hosts down to your team and one other. We've already done the other group's second screen test, and we'd like to schedule your turn," said the voice on the other end. It sounded very unnatural, but in my excitement, any voice could have sounded unusual.

"We want you to come this evening to the vacant house by the old cemetery. We think it will create a more natural setting to see our new program hosts in action," the voice continued.

"What time do we need to be there?" I asked.

"After dark. Don't come until after dark. We'll tell you all you need to know once you get there. Goodbye." The voice went silent, and then I heard the phone hang up.

Matthew's face was shining with happiness, and he asked, "That was the studio, wasn't it?"

"Yes. They want us to go to that weird house by the old cemetery. He said it would be a more natural setting for our next screen test," I said, a little confused. "I don't like that. Everyone says that place is haunted. Even though I know there's no such thing as ghosts, that house is pretty spooky.

"And Matthew, they want us to get there after dark. I don't even like walking past that house in the daytime. Now I have to walk into it at night."

"Are you sure that's where we're supposed to go?" Matthew asked.

"Positive, but something's bothering me. Something about that voice," I said.

"If this thing is bothering you, then what do we do?"

"Tell the others about the next screen test, but don't mention my fear," I told him. He agreed with me, and we called the others and told them to meet us at my house.

By the time the others arrived, the sun was setting. My mom was still not home. I left a note for her, and we started out the front door. Matthew grabbed my shoulder and asked, "Hey, could we pray before we do this? I'm feeling a little scared."

"So am I," Kari added.

I nodded agreement, but Juan almost didn't hear us. He was so intent on getting to the old house and doing a great job at the test that he didn't notice we'd stopped. Matthew called to get Juan's attention, and he turned. "Come on, I don't want to miss this chance," he said when he saw us standing still.

I looked at him with a serious gaze, "We wanted to pray first."

"Sorry, that's a great idea. Could I pray for us?" he asked.

We all nodded our heads. Juan bowed his head and closed his eyes. Kari, Matthew, and I followed his lead. Then he began to pray, "Father in heaven, I want to ask for your protection on us. I wouldn't mind it if a few of your angels could hang out with us. Keep us cool when we need it. And don't let us do anything really stupid. We pray in Jesus' name, amen."

He looked up at us and smiled. I smiled back as I thought about how Juan had changed in the last year. It had started at summer camp. The counselor had spent a lot of time with Juan. They studied the Bible together each morning and prayed together each evening. It had a great effect on Juan. He had become the spiritual leader in our youth group. Even as crazy as he can be, Juan had grown strong in his faith.

After his prayer, we all felt better about heading to the old house. As we walked, I could feel the wind blasting down the street and heard it whistling between the houses. I said to the others, "What a great night for visiting a haunted house. The wind is blowing and howling. All we need now is lightning to make the evening perfect."

As if on cue, thunder cracked in the distance and

a bolt of lightning danced its jagged edges through the sky.

"That was spooky," Kari said.

"I hope that isn't a sign of what the rest of the night is going to be like. I want to be the host of a monster show, not the victim of a monster's appetite," Matthew chipped in.

The wind suddenly grew stronger. I heard the clank of a garbage can being knocked over. In a moment it rolled down a stony driveway. We all looked in the direction of the noise when Kari let out a shriek.

I turned in time to see her being engulfed by a dark shape.

Matthew leaped to her aid. "Don't worry Kari, I, Mattman, doer of good and fighter of evil, will keep that plastic garbage bag from harming you."

Matthew grabbed it from Kari's back and pretended to fight with it. He fell to the ground with it on him. He rolled over, jumped to his feet, and stomped on it. "Take that, evil villain!"

By the time he was done, Kari, Juan, and I were falling to the ground with laughter. I think that's why I liked hanging out with these three. We could always laugh at the scary times and pray together in good and bad times. I think that's what friends are for.

We picked ourselves up and started walking toward the old cemetery again. The house sat near it. I think it once belonged to the man who took care of the lawn at the cemetery. He had died and was buried there, but they never found someone to take his job. The graves were often overgrown with weeds. It really is a creepy place. I tried to avoid it as much as I could. But tonight, it wasn't just the cemetery we had to go through. We had to go in the house as well.

We turned the corner onto Eerie Street. There was the house at the end of it. I've always thought it was fitting that our town's only haunted house sat on a street named Eerie.

With each step, we got closer to the house and moved closer to each other. If the others felt like I did, then I wasn't sure how we'd get through the screen test.

It was the first time that I ever really looked at the house. It was surrounded by a stone wall that had a metal gate in the middle of it. The gate opened to a walkway that led to the front porch and door. To the left of the house, there was another walkway that ended at a gate to the backyard. The house badly needed painting.

I was lost in studying the house when Kari said, "That's strange."

"You can say that again. This place really looks strange," I responded.

"No, that's not what I'm talking about. If we're supposed to be having a screen test here, then there ought to be cars in the driveway." She sounded very puzzled.

Juan offered a few reasons. "Kari, you think too much. Their cars could be in the garage. Their cars could be around back. They could all be running a little late. You're too suspicious about things."

"That's why I get into fewer jams than you three. I always look before I leap," she fired back.

"Does that mean that I don't?" Juan asked, a little put out.

"Hold it! We're here to show how well we work together, remember? They don't want to see how well we fight," Matthew pointed out.

"He's right, Kari, I'm sorry," Juan apologized.

"The same from me," she responded.

I grabbed their hands to gather us all together and said, "Since we're over our little fight, why don't we enter through this gate?" I looked around at them. They were expecting me to come up with the next move, so I made it.

I turned and walked directly toward the metal gate and pulled on the handle. It was very heavy and hard to move. The others pitched in and we got it open.

We moved through the gate's opening very slowly. It was just beginning to get dark. There was no reason to disturb anything that lurked beyond that stone border. First, Kari went through. Juan was right behind her and then Matthew. I followed quietly.

"This is some creepy place," Matthew said as we all looked up at the dark face of the house. The two gabled windows above seemed to stare out at us like sightless eyes, while the doorway resembled a gaping

34

mouth. The webbing of cracks in the paint gave the whole house a wrinkled and aged appearance.

We stood there for a few seconds until the sound of the heavy gate banging closed behind us made us jump.

Kari shrieked as she jumped. I turned and saw that the gate had slammed and locked itself. On the inside of the gate was a sign that read, "Trespassers Beware!" Why wasn't it posted on the outside?

I turned to tell the others about the sign, but they were gone. My eye caught a flash of movement as they hustled around the corner of the house to explore. I didn't want to stand there reading signs on gates all by myself, so I took off running to catch up.

I got to them as they came to the other gate leading into the backyard. Matthew examined the gate. Juan was looking at the house as Kari tried to peer in the garage window to see if there was any sign of a camera crew.

When I caught my breath, I said, "Thanks for waiting around for me. If there had been a monster behind us I'd be a food choice at Monster Middle School." I don't think they even heard me. They all looked intent on what they were doing.

"There's nothing in the garage," Kari turned to me and said. "No cars, no cameras. There is something under a tarp, but I don't think a cameraman would tarp his car in a garage for a few hours' work."

Maybe they forgot a piece of equipment and sent someone back to the studio in the van," I suggested.

"I still say they're probably just running late," said Juan.

"Hey," Matthew interrupted our little guessing game. "This gate is unlocked. Are we ready to take the next step to become the new hosts of *Tales of Terror*?"

In unison we nodded a frightened yes.

Matthew turned to the gate and pulled it open. The back of the house was even spookier-looking than the front. A dim streetlight shone into the yard. We could see old gravestones everywhere. Some had toppled over. It was the spookiest cemetery I had ever seen.

As the others moved forward, I stopped to whisper a prayer to the Lord, "What are we getting into, Father? Something doesn't feel right. Protect us from doing anything stupid."

Matthew whispered, "I don't remember the graves being so close to the house. These stones are in the backyard. My dad didn't tell me about them when he told his stories about this graveyard. You know, there's an old legend about this cemetery."

"Come on, that's what everybody says about the graveyards in their towns," Juan responded.

"I believe this one. My grandfather said it happened when he was a little boy, and my dad says he saw it too," Matthew answered.

"So?" Kari said.

"So, it's a pretty frightening story," he said.

"Just tell it. I think we all want to hear it, even though it will most likely scare us until our hair stands on end," Kari said.

"Okay, you asked for it. About seventy years ago, there was a horrible train accident not too far from the cemetery. The old tracks are just on the other side of those trees. An old deaf woman who lived nearby was involved. I never could find out exactly where she lived. My dad just said that she lived near the cemetery. It could even be this house.

"One evening her cat got away, and she went to find it. She was scared that something might happen to it on the railroad tracks. She eventually found the cat playing on the tracks. Because she was deaf, she never heard the train coming. It hit them, and she and her cat went flying into the air."

"Oooo, so that's the big scary story?" Juan mocked as he rolled his eyes.

"No, it doesn't end there," Matthew continued. "No one knows what happened to the cat's body. The woman's restless spirit roams the graveyard every night calling for her kitty. My dad even saw her once."

As he said that, something dark rolled between his legs.

Matthew yelped and jumped up on the gravestone he was sitting on. I slapped my hand over my mouth to muffle my cry as Juan dove behind another head-stone. I looked down expecting to see the ghost of the cat. Instead I saw a rubber ball.

I heard a giggle. It was Kari laughing at us. "I couldn't resist getting all of you with that one. If you listen to those kinds of stories and believe them, you deserve to get scared like that. All that stuff isn't logical, and if you remember, it isn't biblical.

"I've done enough research on that project Beth assigned me to know that we don't have to be afraid of stories about dead people's restless spirits roaming graveyards at night," said Kari.

"But the story is true!" Matthew insisted.

"What proof do you have that it's true?" Kari asked. Matthew started to answer, but no words came to his open mouth. He looked like he had seen something that scared him speechless.

I turned around to see what he was looking at, and there was no doubt about it. Walking toward us, in the thick fog that was forming on the old graveyard, was a ghostly woman.

Nothing was going to stop us from getting out of there. The four of us took off with our feet tearing up the dirt and throwing it to the sides. My legs were moving faster than I could control them.

I was only about halfway to the gate, dodging between the gravestones, when I stumbled and fell. I couldn't figure out what tripped me until I heard the others yell. I looked down at my feet. Out of the ground stuck a twisted, decaying hand slowly opening and closing. I screamed, "What is this?"

Kari's eyes were filled with terror. Hands were poking up from every grave. The dead were trying to rise from beneath the withered grass. Or maybe they were trying to take us down into the damp dirt to join them. I wasn't about to become a part of that plan.

I pressed down with my hands and leaped to my feet. I saw that none of the hands came any farther out of the ground than their wrists. All I had to do was avoid getting gripped by those icy, bony fingers that wiggled in the air.

I dodged from one grave to another, but it seemed like the hands knew where I would run next. A hand popped up just to the right of my left foot. I leaped onto the next patch of grass and another shoved its way into the open air. I had been scared before, but this was something different. *Lord, please keep us calm and help us figure out how to get out of here!*

After dodging and weaving I realized I had run in a circle. I wasn't getting any closer to the house or to the gate. I was stuck in a holding pattern above groping, ghostly hands.

The others had the same problem. Kari tried leaping from the top of one tombstone to another. It worked for her first four jumps, but on the fifth one she tumbled to the earth and landed flat on her back. A hand came up an inch from the top of her head and reached for her. She twisted and scrambled as she hurried to get away. Kari never gave up easily. Using a gymnastic move, she jumped from her back to her feet as she pushed with her hands on the ground. It was too much for the graveside gripper. Kari ran free—only to face a dozen more hands as they came popping out of the dirt.

Juan backed up against a high tombstone. It read, "Ronald Clarkson, 1830–1857—His own wicked hands caused his death. He says he'll return, but don't hold your breath." Around Juan was a ring of hands. No matter which way he went, the long-fingered, clenching hands waited for him.

I couldn't see Matthew, but I heard him moving somewhere in the fog. I could see that the ghostly woman had gotten closer. We needed to get out of this place. I finally saw my chance. I took three running steps and leaped onto the highest gravestone. From it, I pushed off into the air. For a brief second I was airborne and clear of the hands.

My body came crashing down just past the last grave. I landed with a thud, and I felt the air rush out of my lungs in a loud "oomph." I had escaped the hands, but what about the ghostly woman?

I forced myself to sit up as I gulped in air. The ghostly creature was still coming slowly toward me in the fog. I was readying myself to stand up when Kari came crashing into the dirt next to me.

She rolled over and said, "I saw what you did, and I did the same. It worked for us, but Juan and Matthew are still too deep inside the graveyard to jump out. What do we do now?"

I looked critically at the graveyard, and a plan came into my mind. Juan only had to climb that tall tombstone and reach the limb above his head. He could pull himself into the tree and jump out of the cemetery from it. I yelled my idea to him.

He grinned in relief as he jumped into the air and

grabbed the limb. In a minute he was standing next to us. "Thanks, Bethany, I would never have thought of that. What about Matthew?" Juan asked.

"The ghost is moving pretty slowly. If we can get Matthew out of there in the next few minutes, we can escape without her grabbing us," Kari told us.

"There is only one problem," I said as I looked around. "Where is Matthew?" It did not take long to get my answer. Out of the fog came Matthew's blood-curdling shriek of terror.

"Where is he?" I yelled.

"It sounds like he's behind that mausoleum over there," Kari cried back to me.

"At least we don't have to worry about getting grabbed anymore. It looks like the hands have all gone back into their graves," Juan said.

"Then what are we standing here for? Let's go save our friend!" Kari was already running as she finished her plea for action. Juan and I bolted behind her, and she led us toward the other side of the mausoleum.

As Juan and I rounded the corner of the above-ground tomb, we nearly crashed into Kari. She was standing over an open grave. I skidded to a stop in loose dirt next to her, causing some of the dirt to go sliding into the deep hole.

I looked down. Matthew had fallen into the empty grave! I scanned the area for something we could use to pull him out. I didn't see anything useful. But I did see that the ghostly woman was continuing her evening stroll our way.

Matthew looked up at us and smiled. He said, "Isn't there something in the Bible about Joseph being thrown into a hole in the ground?"

Kari snapped, "This is no time for a Bible lesson."

"Actually, it is. Right now, I need all of my faith to get me through this," he countered. He was trying his best to remain calm.

"Listen, we have about three minutes to get Matthew out of there before that woman joins him," I said. "I suggest we do something now."

"All he has to do is step on that, and we can reach his hands to pull him out," Juan told us as he pointed at the side of the freshly dug hole. I saw four little fingers wiggling their way out of the dirt.

Matthew turned toward them. I didn't have to see his eyes to know that he was scared. He took a step back, but Kari stopped him.

"Don't move, Matthew! There are fingers poking out of the dirt behind you too," she called.

Juan took over. "Matthew, I've got an idea. It's going to sound like the stupidest thing you ever heard, but if you do what I say, I think we can get you out of there."

Matthew nodded his agreement.

Juan continued, "The three of us are going to lie in the dirt above that hand in front of you. I want you to help it get free of the dirt. The moment its palm pokes through, run toward it and jump. Use it like a step. We'll grab your hand and you're out."

"You're right. It is a stupid idea, but I don't hear any smart ones," Matthew said as he agreed to try it. He freed the fingers, and then the hand came out. Before it could twist and grab for him, Matthew backed up, ran toward it, and jumped. All three of us grabbed his hands and pulled him out of the hole. He was safe, but were we all really safe? Where was the ghostly woman?

14

I looked in her direction. She was only ten feet away. The four of us stumbled over each other in our attempt to run. Kari fell, and we picked her up. I looked again. The woman was only five feet away. I could see her tattered and torn dress blowing in the wind.

Juan and Kari ran for the gate. Matthew tried to run and realized that he had twisted his ankle. He went down on one knee. I looked at him. Then I looked at the ghostly woman. She was raising her hand to grab me.

Matthew turned his head in time to see her. I don't know whether fear can heal a sprain, but Matthew jumped up and grabbed my hand. He pulled me forward as the creepy fingers of the woman were about to touch my arm.

I went flying after Matthew toward our friends. They pulled and rattled the gate, but it would not budge. Its top had sharp metal spikes, so no one could climb over it. We were stuck. How long could we avoid the woman?

I looked back to see where she was. She had disappeared. We concentrated on getting out of this place.

"Let's get this open and go home," I said.

"How?" came from Matthew.

I looked around and saw an old tool shed. If it was like the one at my house, I would find something in it that we could use to pry the gate open with. I ran to the shed.

I sucked in a deep breath. I wasn't sure what I would find inside, but I had no choice. I reached out and pulled the door open. Nothing got me. The shed was filled with tools. My eyes ran over every corner until I saw a pick with long pointed ends. I was sure that the pick could break through the gate's hinges.

I turned and stood at the shed's opening and held up the pick for my friends to see. It was exactly what we needed. I expected to see smiling faces, but they were covering their mouths with their hands. Their eyes kept growing larger. Something told me that I was in trouble.

I saw the pale, spooky hand of the ghostly woman reach over my shoulder.

I spun around. Cradled in the woman's other arm was her dead cat. She had found it, but unfortunately I did not have the energy to be happy for her. I wanted out of this place.

She spoke to me. Her voice was low and soft. "Turn back! Run away!" The woman turned away from me. She walked into the fog and disappeared.

I did not move for a minute. Fear had turned me into a statue. Then my legs went weak, and I fell to the ground. In a second, Matthew was next to me helping me up. As I rose I grabbed the pick.

"Are you okay, Bethany?" he asked.

"Yes, but I have never been so frightened in my life. The thing that scared me most was when she told me to run away," I told him.

"We better tell the others what she told you," he said as he helped me back to Kari and Juan.

"Bethany said that the ghostly woman spoke to her," Matthew told them.

"She said that we should turn back and run away. I think she was warning us that this place is dangerous," I said in a soft and breathless voice. "Let's get this gate open and get out of here."

"Are you crazy?" Juan asked. "Remember, we came here to do a screen test for *Tales of Terror*. Since this is one of their sets, I'm sure we must have triggered the mechanisms that work the special effects. Everything we saw was probably props and mechanical things that are run by someone behind a control panel."

I did not feel reassured. "Juan, who is running them? We haven't seen any cars or people. I don't think the studio would try to scare us away from being their hosts."

"I guess there is only one way to find out. Let's go inside and look for Mr. Christensen," he told me. The moment he said that the gate clicked and swung slowly open. "See! What did I tell you? Somebody wants us to go back out front and into the house."

We looked at the opening gate. We saw a figure dressed in a black robe and hood walking toward the front of the house. Had he opened the gate?

Juan continued, "That was our invitation. If we want to be the hosts of the show then we have to do this."

I wasn't sure that I agreed with him, but I wanted to be a host of *Tales of Terror*. I followed him.

As we walked toward the house, Matthew said,

"That cemetery was really strange. I felt like I was living a really scary movie."

"*Hands of the Dead* to be exact," Kari responded.

"Yeah, that's it, Kari. I remember that old black-and-white horror movie on *Tales of Terror.* The hosts did their part from a graveyard where hands popped out of the ground. Juan is right. We must have wandered into one of their scenes and triggered the special effects," Matthew told us.

Sure that we were in the middle of the screen test, we stopped near the front steps. I wanted to check the front gate. I tugged on it. As I expected, it wouldn't move. We had to enter the house and find out what was going on.

"Any luck?" Kari asked.

"No, I guess our only choice is to go in," I responded.

"That is exactly what I said," Juan gloated.

We climbed the creaking steps. I was afraid we would fall through, but we made it safely. I was in the front of our little group. We all stared at the door.

Juan interrupted my thoughts, "Bethany, it isn't going to open itself. Just twist the knob so we can get in."

I tried it. The door was locked. A wave of relief rippled from the top of my head to my feet. I smiled and turned around. I was ready to leave, but Juan pushed by me.

He said, "If it's locked, we'll just have to ring the doorbell."

He reached up and pushed the button. The bell sounded like the deep foghorn on that old comedy, *The Munsters*. The sound made us laugh.

"I guess our ghosts watch TV and have a sense of humor," Matthew said between his giggles.

Kari stopped our laughing when she pointed at the door. It was slowly opening all by itself.

We looked inside. The entry was dark and smelled like an old closet. This was not the kind of place that I would pick for a vacation. I wouldn't even pick it for a TV studio set. It looked really spooky.

We walked through the doorway into a giant foyer. Above us hung a large glass chandelier. Cobwebs stretched from the light to the wall above the door. I could barely see the wide staircase with the winding railing in front of us. It looked like every haunted house set I had ever seen.

"Hello, is anybody home?" I called out.

No response. No noise at all.

"It's dead silent in here," Juan said.

"Don't use that word," said Matthew.

"What word?" questioned Juan.

"Dead!"

I agreed. I could feel us all tense up when he said it. But this place *was* dead silent, and that made me uncomfortable—very uncomfortable.

Juan turned to us and said, "We need to find out what's going on. I suggest we split up and search the place. That way we can finish this screen test and get home. There's a great scary movie on TV tonight that I want to see."

"I've had enough scary stuff for one day," I said. "And I don't want to split up. Every time we've gotten into a tough spot it took more than one of us to get out of it. I say we stay together."

"I agree with Bethany, and since I have the only flashlight, I'll be our leader," Kari said.

"Where's your flashlight?" Matthew asked.

"On my key chain," she said as she showed us. It was a small yellow one with soft sides. As long as you squeezed it, the light stayed on.

"That won't last long," Juan said. "We need a candle or something. Let's see what we can find." He walked toward the big room to our left. I went straight ahead, but it was too dark to see anything clearly. I could barely even see my feet. Kari's flashlight was shining on the stairway.

"Juan, where are you?" I called.

Juan answered, "If I could see, I would know where I was. This looks like some kind of dining room. Hey, I just touched some stones. It must be a fireplace."

"Great. Can you find some matches or a candle?" Kari asked.

"If you can shine your teeny, tiny flashlight this way, I'll see what's here," he called back to her.

Kari moved toward the room that Juan was in. Matthew and I migrated her way. Juan's gasp made Kari stop in the doorway.

"Juan, are you all right?" Kari called.

"Yeah, I'm okay, but there is some kind of sticky web stuff all over me. Hurry up and help me get out of this stuff. I feel too much like little Miss Muffet waiting for the spider to come her way," he said.

Kari moved into the room searching for him. The beam of light danced along the floor searching for Juan. We found him trapped in what looked like a huge spider web. I almost laughed. Then Kari's flashlight beam hit the ceiling.

Juan and I saw the spider at the same time. I gasped, but he almost whimpered, "Hurry up, this thing looks like it hasn't eaten in a while."

We all stared at the ceiling. Kari's light made it easy to see the huge eight-legged hunter. It had to be at least as big as we were. The spider crawled slowly toward the wall. I was glad that it didn't drop its webbing down on us. We could all be trapped.

Matthew was tearing at the web. He had freed

Juan's head and was moving toward his shoulders and arms. I watched the progress of the spider. At the rate Matthew was going, Juan would end up as tonight's main course for the spider's dinner.

"Can't you rip any faster?" Kari cried to Matthew.

"Hurry up and free my arms so I can help get this stuff off me," Juan added. He turned toward me and asked urgently, "Bethany, could you lend a hand instead of watching the spider?"

I reached down and started pulling at the web on his feet. It was very sticky. As soon as I ripped a handful away, the remaining web closed up on itself.

"Can you get some light on Juan so we can see what we're doing?" I asked.

"Please hurry. I can see the spider moving across the ceiling. He's about six inches from the wall," Juan cried out.

We tore the webbing away from Juan's body a small section at a time. It was slow going, and every time we turned our heads to look at the spider creeping toward Juan, it slowed us more.

The spider reached the wall and was heading toward the floor. I didn't like the looks of it. The hairy body seemed larger as it walked down the wall. Kari lit the spider once with her flashlight, and I was sure that its mouth was opening and closing. It would only take another minute for the beast to reach us. I prayed we would free Juan by then.

The handfuls of web we yanked away felt like a thick sticky string. Finally Juan's right leg was loose.

I glanced at the spider from the corner of my eye. It was so close! We had only seconds. When I looked back Juan had freed his other leg and jumped to his feet.

"I'm free! Let's get out of here," Juan yelled to us. He flew past me, and Kari was right behind. The light beam bounced along the floor to guide them. As Matthew ran past me, he grabbed my arm and tried to pull me with him. I tripped on a pile of the sticky webbing. I went sprawling across the floor and ended up tangled in the web only inches from the mouth of the spider.

"Help!" I yelled. I saw Matthew and Kari turn my way. Kari splashed her light on my face. I knew they could see the fear sweeping over it.

The spider reached for me. My legs were cemented to the floor, but my upper body was free. I twisted away from the hairy legs. At the same time, Matthew freed my feet. I stood up quickly. The stringy goo clung to my legs, but I could run.

"Let's get out of this crazy place. I don't think I want to be a host on this show if we have to do stuff like this," I told my friends.

Kari agreed. "I'm out of here." She turned the flashlight beam and passed it over the door.

Juan slowly turned to us and said, "It looks like none of us are getting out of here."

I ran to the door and rattled the iron bars that had mysteriously blocked the exit, but it was hopeless. "Forget this way. We need to find another door before the spider comes looking for us."

Matthew crept back toward the dining room. He stuck his head inside. "It's gone. The spider must have found a better meal elsewhere."

Juan was relieved and started to joke with Matthew, "I'm sure I'm too skinny to make a good meal. That's why it gave up."

"Well then, Bones, can you tell us what we should do next?" Kari asked him as she jammed her hands on her hips.

"Let's explore this place. I'm not sure that the whole web and spider bit wasn't just special effects. Let's look around," he told us.

"I think Juan might be right. I never saw the hosts on *Tales of Terror* face down a spider, but a similar scene happened in *Revenge of the Science Project*," Matthew said.

"Maybe it was only a movie scene," Kari said, "but I want out of here. Juan, how could you want to explore this place? Five minutes ago you were almost a Juanburger and wanted out of here."

"I don't think we have any choice but to explore. Our only way out is barred," he answered.

"I'm afraid Juan's right," I told the other two. "Kari has the flashlight. As long as it lasts, we can see where we're going."

"Then we're in worse trouble than we thought. Those flashlights will last only an hour or so. What if we're stuck in here all night?" Juan asked us.

Matthew raised his hand like a kid does in the middle of a school class. "What we need are some matches and a candle. Anybody seen any?"

I frowned. "Look around in the furniture. Maybe there are some matches or something in one of the drawers," I directed the others. With only the weak glow of Kari's flashlight to guide us, we spread out to search. Juan found a candle on a table, but we still needed matches. We started to open the doors and drawers of the antiques that filled the room.

Kari stood behind us flashing her light into each opening. I held my breath every time I pulled a drawer open. I expected to see a spider or bones from something. Instead, I found nothing. Each drawer was more than suspiciously empty. It was like the furniture was never intended to be used.

I heard Matthew call out, "Kari, bring the light closer. I think I see something in this desk." He shoved his hand into a long drawer. He kept feeling around. Suddenly he let out a shriek that sent chills up and down my spine.

Matthew pulled his hand quickly from the drawer. Kari's flashlight lit it up, and we saw that one of his fingers was missing. Her light went to his face. Matthew's features were twisted and contorted in agony. He fell to his knees.

Juan was the first to reach Matthew.

While Juan helped our friend, I yelled to Kari, "Shine the light in the drawer. I want to see if I can find his finger. We might be able to get it to a hospital and have it sewn back on." Touching a bloody, severed finger was the last thing I wanted to do, but for my friend I knew I had to.

Kari's light panned back and forth inside the drawer. There wasn't a finger. There wasn't even any blood. Not a drop anywhere.

I didn't have time to say a word before Matthew stood up and whispered to us, "I am starting to feel strange. Something is taking over my mind. I've become one of the . . ."

". . . thirsty dead," Juan finished. "That was a stupid trick when the kid did it in the movie called *The Thirsty Dead,* and it is still a stupid trick."

"He was faking it? Matthew, I can't believe you

63

would sink to such a thing, especially when we've already been so scared," I said in disappointment.

"We all laughed when we saw it in the movie," he said, trying to defend himself.

"That was the movies, and if you remember, living through a movie scene is not much fun in this place. This is us standing in a haunted house with all the doors blocked off. This is not the time to play 'fake-out,'" I tossed back at him. "Just make up for being a jerk by finding some matches."

As I said that I turned and pulled open another drawer in the same desk. Something flew right toward my face.

19

Juan looked at me when I jumped back in fright and asked, "Did you lose a finger as well?"

"No, there was something inside the drawer, and it leaped out at me," I got out between my gasps. "Look, there it is on the floor."

Matthew moved toward the dark shadow on the floor. He got closer, and it scurried in the direction of Juan. Juan jumped at it, and it ran at Kari.

Kari turned her light in the direction of the spot. "It's just a mouse," she scoffed.

"How could I know it was just a mouse?" I told the others.

"Well, it was nothing. Let's concentrate on finding some matches," Matthew said as Kari's flashlight blinked. Then the beam started to lose its strength.

Juan jumped at Kari and pulled the flashlight from her hand. "We need to conserve the battery," he said.

"We need to find matches and the only way to do that is by using the flashlight," Kari argued.

I suggested, "Let's shine the light quickly into each drawer. There are only a few more." I walked over to a really strange looking machine. The moon cut through a spot in the window, giving me enough light to examine it. I lifted the top. Inside it almost looked like an old record player. "What is this?" I whispered to Kari.

Looking over my shoulder, she said, "That's an old gramophone."

"What kind of grandmother was that?"

"Not a grandmother," she said, laughing. "I saw one in a museum once. It is kind of like an old stereo. It uses these black things that look like cans to play music. The quality wasn't that good. Not even rap could sound good on that thing." She giggled at her own joke and went to the closet next to the old music machine.

I wasn't sure that I believed the black cans could make music. I picked one up as Juan and Matthew started feeling their way along the wall. The little bit of moonlight that was sneaking in the windows didn't reach the far end of the room. I heard them stumble over things.

"Are you two okay?" I asked.

"We're fine," Matthew said.

"My shins aren't fine," Juan added. And then he asked, "Kari, could you shine the light over here for a second?"

She pointed it their way, but the beam was getting so weak it did not reach. "It's going fast. We need to pray that we'll find some matches on this side of the room," she said, disappointed.

I picked up the black can that made music, and Kari opened the closet door at the same time. Out of my little can fell some matches—out of Kari's closet fell a body.

Kari screamed and started running from the room. Right behind her went Matthew and Juan. But to join my friends, I had to leap over the body.

At first, I was too frightened to look down, but if I had any hope of surviving this trip through the haunted house I had to. I held my breath and glanced down. In the dark, with only a little moonlight, it was hard to tell what was there.

It looked like a man dressed in a suit. If it were a man though, he was very thin. In fact, he was nonexistent. My friends had run because a man's suit had fallen out of a closet.

"Hey, 'fraidy cats! You can come back now. It was only an empty suit of clothes. Come back. I found some matches," I yelled. I could hear their tennis shoes squeak on the wood floor as they returned.

As they reentered the room, Juan and Matthew were pushing each other. "You were the one who was scared. I just followed you," Matthew insisted.

"I was trying to lead you to another room so we could look for matches. If that had been a real body, I would have stuck around to investigate," Juan countered.

Kari joined in, "What is the big deal? So we got scared. Just about everything in this weird place makes me scared. I think being scared has been the only thing that has kept us safe. Fear isn't such a bad thing if it protects you from danger."

"I guess we don't have to go to church this week," Juan said.

Matthew set Juan up for the punch line, "Why not, Juan?"

"Kari already gave us the sermon." Juan was laughing as he said his joke. He then held out the candle so I could light it. The flame threw dancing yellow and orange patterns on the walls.

Matthew started talking, "Now that we have some light, we need to find a way out of here."

"No way!" Juan protested. "I want to be the host of *Tales of Terror*, and we are going to make it through the test in this haunted house."

"How is something like this a screen test?" I argued with him.

"Did you think that what happened at the studio was a screen test?" Juan asked.

I thought for a moment. He was right. Nothing had been what I'd believed it to be. If we gave up now, we'd end our screen test and our chance at being the new hosts.

Juan moved in the direction of the dining room again. Matthew stopped him by grabbing his shoulder and turning his body around. "Why are we going back in there?"

"I've got to see that web. I'd like to know exactly what it is. If I can't figure that out, then I want to see what else is in the room. Who knows, maybe the ghosts that haunt this house have left us some tasty morsels on the dining room table," he answered.

Kari was right behind him. She offered, "Maybe there is some Cream of Eyeball soup."

"That sounds terrible," I told her.

As we entered the dining room I quietly prayed, "Lord, if we are in the middle of a screen test, please bring it to an end soon. This whole place is scaring me. I don't know what's in the room or even what we're about to discover. Please check things out and protect us."

I could see for the first time how big the room was. One end had a sitting area, and the other had a large dining table. "Look at that!" Matthew directed our attention. "It looks like there really is food on the table."

As we got closer and the candlelight shone on the dishes, we could see food still on them. Something large filled a platter in the middle of the table. Everything was covered in thick gray cobwebs. The table had been sitting like this for many years.

I took a few steps closer. Kari stood next to me. We were both staring at the food and wondering what it had been.

"I've got to see this up close," Kari told me. She walked up to the table and stood next to it. Her back was toward me while she continued to speak. "It is real food, but it has certainly seen better days."

"It looks like the guests got up and ran out," I told her.

Kari turned around and bumped one of the chairs. She looked at it, and then looked at me. Somehow she managed to say very calmly, "No, they didn't run out. They are still here."

The words had barely escaped her mouth when a skeleton tipped and hung over the side of the chair. The bony hand hit Kari's leg. I watched as her eyes began rolling back in her head. Kari was ready to faint.

Suddenly the skeleton's skull came loose and bounced at her feet. Kari's knees collapsed, and she fell to the floor into the shadows.

"Kari, are you okay? Get that candle over here, now!" I commanded.

I did not need to say a word. Juan had the candle shining over my shoulder as he bent down to look under the table. Where was Kari? She had to be under there somewhere. It was really spooky looking at the tattered, dusty clothing that clung to the leg bones of the skeletons underneath the table. Spookier still, there was no sign of Kari. Juan and I pulled our heads out from under the table and stood up.

"Where is she?" Matthew asked us. Juan and I shrugged our shoulders to say that we did not know. "What was under there? Where could she have gone? She fell only a few moments ago. If she disappeared she must have been captured."

"Captured by what?" I scoffed.

"I don't know. It could be anything in this place. I'm beginning to think that we wandered into a real haunted house. Maybe this isn't some TV show. Maybe all these frightening things are real. I want out of here," Juan said as fear filled his eyes.

Matthew looked at us both and said, "Wait. I think I saw this whole scene on TV. Juan, I'm getting the feeling that we just may be in a TV show."

"What happened in the show?" I asked.

"I can't remember, but Kari has to be here somewhere. I wonder what's on the other side of the table. It looks like a curtain to me. She probably fainted and rolled behind the curtain."

I hoped he was right. It sounded logical. My mom always told me to look for a logical explanation when something scared me. Was this just a TV show that we walked into? I wasn't sure, but I was positive that God would guide us through it. I had to trust him with each step we took.

Juan swept back the curtain with his hand. I waited to see Kari or a window so we could escape. Either would be nice, but what I saw didn't encourage me. The black velvet curtain covered a window that had been bricked up. There would be no escaping from there.

"What now?" Matthew asked with disappointment in his voice.

"We keep looking," I told him.

"I'm going to check all around this table. There has to be some clue that will lead us to Kari," Juan reported. As he turned to look under the table from the other side, we heard a moan coming from the foyer.

"It's Kari!" I screamed with excitement.

We couldn't run because we needed the candle for light, but when we entered the foyer I saw Kari. She was sprawled out in the middle of the floor and moaning something. When I got closer I could hear what she was saying.

"No, let me go. Let me go!" she mumbled.

Matthew stepped close to her and shook her awake. Kari's eyes opened up, and she shot a relieved smile at us. "I'm so glad it's you three. All I remember is seeing a skull bounce in front of me, and it felt like a bunch of hands pulled me down somewhere. It was so much like a dream that I'm sure that is exactly what it was," she said. Her eyes stared around her and she asked a question, "Where am I? This isn't the dining room."

"What happened may have been for real," I told her. Kari's mouth dropped open. I continued, "When you fell, you rolled under the table and we couldn't see you. You just disappeared. Somehow you got in here, but we don't know how."

All I could do was scratch my head. Not one of us knew what had happened. It was like everything else in this haunted house. Weird things occurred, and I didn't know what was causing them. I really had to cling to the belief that God was going to get us through no matter what.

Juan put his finger to his lips, "Shh." All of us became as quiet as stones and just as still. "Did you hear that?" Juan whispered.

We heard the faint sound of footsteps. We listened for a moment. Then I whispered, "Where are the footsteps coming from?"

Kari answered, "It sounds like the dining room, but it must be upstairs. Nothing in the dining room can walk."

"It could be the spider," Matthew said.

"Or one of the skeletons," I added.

"Or the suit of clothes," Juan said to join in with us, even though he was turned away from us and staring off into the dark.

Kari stopped us, "No, it couldn't be any of those. None of them walk on two feet."

"Want to bet?" Juan asked with a voice that sounded very strange. We all looked at him. He pointed to the suit of clothes. "There is our source of the footsteps." The suit was no longer lying on the floor. Now it strolled across the floor like it was off for its after-dinner walk.

As if the only thing missing had to show up, outside it suddenly started to thunder. The lightning gave us a good view of the walking rags.

We pasted our backs to the wall behind us as the

empty clothing came into the foyer. I was scared when the next two steps were in our direction.

The suit stopped and swiveled its empty form in our direction. Then it started to walk again. I felt the sweat start on my forehead and then creep down my face. At the same time, my cold hands went wet and clammy. I was scared. I was very scared.

Suddenly the suit turned away from us and began climbing the staircase. After taking three steps, it stopped and turned just slightly toward us again. I was sure I saw one shoulder give a little twitch as if to signal to us that the suit expected us to follow it up the stairs.

Juan moved close to the suit with the candle in his hand and motioned for us to follow. "If we don't follow, then we won't know where it is going. That suit knows something that we don't. Let's go!"

A few minutes ago, Juan was as scared as I was. Now, he and Kari were leaping the steps two at a time to keep up with the empty clothing. Matthew and I moved more cautiously. I wanted to find a way out of here, but there was nothing written anywhere that said, "an empty suit of clothing will lead them."

The suit reached the top of the stairs and turned right. It kept going down the hallway to the door at the end. The door swung open, but no hand had reached out to open it. The empty suit of clothing walked through the doorway, and the door glided shut.

Juan called to us, "We've got to get in there fast and see where it goes. Catch up to us." Then he took off running down the hall, protecting the flame with his hand. We caught up as he reached the door.

Kari did not even wait for someone to encourage her to open the door. She twisted the handle and pushed it open. The candle's flame threw enough light inside for me to see that the suit of clothing was gone, but I did catch a glimpse of wall panel sliding shut.

"Where did it go?" Matthew asked.

"Through that wall," Kari said as she and Juan entered the room. "We'll have to follow it into that secret passageway."

Matthew and I stepped inside. He said to us, "*It Walks at Night.*"

"Once again, you are the king of the obvious," Juan said.

"No, I mean that was the name of the movie that scene came from," he answered. "We just walked into the rest of the scene."

I held my breath and let go of the door that I was holding open. It started to slam shut like it was pulled by a vacuum.

"We don't want to get trapped inside this room," he added.

I dove for the handle on the door to keep it from closing. When I grabbed the knob, it fell off in my hand. I turned around to tell the others that we were in trouble because we could not get out. But that was the least of our problems.

The walls turned into thousands of rapidly blinking lights, like tiny strobe lights. It made each movement look like it was in slow motion. I found it hard to make my way to the other three. With each blink of the lights, I lost my focus on where they were.

"Everybody stop so I can catch up to you," I yelled, but it did no good. Along with the blinking lights, loud sounds like monster growls from cheap horror movies rained down on us. My friends could not hear a word I said.

The lights and the sounds confused me. I was so mixed up that I was sure there were monsters starting to circle us. I saw to my left the snarling lips and long teeth of a beast with green bumpy skin. Its long-clawed paw reached out for me. I ducked.

When I looked up again, it was gone, but there was another one moving toward me. Drool escaped its mouth as the hairy, creepy thing licked its thin, scaly lips. It reached for me. I leaped to the right and rolled on the floor. The sounds and the lights made it very difficult to see exactly where I was. I stood up and nearly knocked Juan over.

"What's going on?" I screamed in his ear.

"I can't understand it. The monsters get close, and then they disappear into thin air. The hands never get close enough to reach us," Juan yelled back as he leaned in about an inch from my ear.

"They aren't real, are they?" I concluded. It was a false feeling of safety. I barely turned my mouth away from Juan when I felt something grip my shoulder. "Ahh!" I shrieked and spun around.

"Bethany, this is really weird," Matthew yelled when he turned me around.

"You scared me," I screamed at him.

"Sorry, but we have got to get out of here."

"How?" I asked. "The door we came in is stuck shut, and there isn't a knob on the inside. The only way out is the way the suit of clothes went."

"We don't have much of a choice, do we?" Kari yelled as she moved closer to us. "I'm heading for the wall now."

Matthew and I grabbed onto her, and the three of us walked steadily to the wall where the secret door was. Juan was already at the secret door. He felt around for a trip switch. Then his hand touched something, and the wall slid back.

The blinking lights allowed us to see inside the

secret passageway. It looked like a hallway and nothing else. Juan entered and Kari followed. I looked at Matthew, and he gestured for me to go before him. I gestured back for him to go. Then I realized that I did not want to be the last one in the room in case the wall slid back before I made it through. I jumped across the threshold and pulled Matthew with me.

I stood inside the passageway, quickly closed my eyes, and spoke to the Lord. "Each step gets us deeper into this house. I'm really afraid. I'm not sure I want this stupid TV host job. I'm ready to get out of here fast."

The door shut, and the sound was cut off. Juan struck another match to relight our candle and said, "We don't have much choice. We could go back through the wall and into the monster room or down this hallway."

I looked at the wall. There wasn't any way to open the secret sliding door. "I'm afraid we only have one way to go and that is down the hall. The wall is solidly in place and there isn't any way back out."

"Let's go," Kari commanded.

We walked slowly through the passageway. I noticed that the ceiling got closer and closer to my head. Juan did also. He turned around and whispered, "Either I'm going through an amazing growth spurt or this passageway is getting lower with each step we take."

"I wish it was rapid growth, but the ceiling is getting lower as we go. I think the walls are getting closer too," Matthew added.

"I feel like we need to stop and pray before anything else goes wrong," I said.

"I've been praying since we got in here," Matthew responded. "I'll keep it up as we go along."

"I feel better," I told him.

The hallway kept closing in on us. We were starting to walk in a crouched position. After only a few feet of walking like that, we had to drop to our knees. The passage got tighter and tighter.

It felt like the walls were squeezing me. It was not a nice feeling. I said to the others, "It is really hard to breathe in here. This is getting bad."

"It just got worse," Juan called from the front.

"What's wrong?" Kari questioned.

"The passageway just ended," he said.

"We better go back," Kari suggested.

"Back to what? The wall panel didn't have a handle or catch on the inside," I reminded her.

"I was just thinking," Matthew said.

"Oh, *that's* what I smell," Juan teased. "I thought it was just your old sneakers." Juan's joke was an attempt to relieve our tension, but it fell flat.

"Stop it, Juan!" I said sternly. "Tell us what you were thinking, Matthew."

"If the suit of clothes could come in here and then get out, there must be another exit," he stated.

"Not a bad theory," Kari responded. "Except that if it is a ghost then it could pass right through the walls."

"It wasn't a ghost, or it would have passed through the door without opening it. It wasn't a ghost in the movie either. Besides, I don't believe in ghosts. Do you?" Matthew said.

"I didn't, but maybe I need to reconsider the possibility," I muttered under my breath. Then louder I said, "It is hot in here, and I don't like to be closed in."

"At least it isn't dark," Juan said, but he said it just a fraction of a second too soon. The candle flame was puffed out by a blast of air. "Me and my big mouth," Juan added.

"We have got to go back," Kari said.

"I don't think so," I told them. "Listen, I think we've got company coming."

We heard a low growling and the sound of claws scraping along the passageway floor. We were all silent as the sounds came closer. I was holding my breath.

"I don't think coming in here was such a good idea," Kari told Juan. "We're trapped."

The approaching sound continued growing louder. In a few seconds we could be eaten alive. The others started to shake from fear. They shook so hard that I could feel the floor vibrate.

"Who is shaking?" Matthew asked.

"It's the floor. It's moving," Juan yelled.

One moment I was preparing to be a monster meal, and the next I was hurdling down a long slide. We screamed and shrieked as our bodies flew to the bottom. I prayed that there would be something soft to land on.

I could see dim light ahead. First Juan dropped from the hole. Behind him was Kari and then me. I did have something soft to land on: Juan and Kari. Matthew had something even softer. After I was added to the cushion below, he popped out and came tumbling on top of us.

"Oomph!" we all yelled.

Our bodies tangled in a pile of legs and arms. I tried pulling away, but couldn't move. "Hey, Matthew. You have to get up first," I told him.

"Where are we?" he asked groggily.

"So far, all I've seen are various body parts of others where I expect to see my own body parts," Kari groaned from beneath me. "I have no idea where we are, but if we all get up, I'm sure we can find out."

Matthew and I climbed off Kari and Juan. We stood up and extended our hands to Kari and pulled her up. Juan lay still. Kari lightly kicked him and said, "Juan don't mess around. We're already scared enough."

Juan did not respond at first. I bent down and saw that he was starting to stir. He groaned out, "What happened?"

"We all landed on you. Are you all right?" I asked.

"I think so, but my head feels kind of groggy. Where are we?" he asked.

Kari had been looking around and answered, "I see one bare light bulb swinging from the ceiling. The walls are made of stone, and it smells like a damp basement, so I presume we are in a basement."

"Thank you, Nancy Drew," Matthew said.

"Well, you asked. I just told you what I saw and

smelled, but I did not tell you what I heard," she said in a snooty voice. "I hear something else, and it does not sound like a friendly little house cat."

As she said that I saw a shadow appear on the stone wall behind her. It was like no other shadow I had ever seen before. It was a beast with two heads. One of them was long and thin with two antennae on the top. The other was flat and wide, and it looked like there were fish gills flapping on the sides of it.

When they turned their heads to the side, I could see the shadows of their tongues lash out like snakes' and lick the air. I got the impression that the two-headed beast was trying to get a taste of us to see if we would make a good meal.

I yelled to the others, "Look at the wall! I can see the shadow of a two-headed monster."

"The shadow is getting bigger. That means it's getting closer to us," Matthew spit out.

"I don't see anything but a shadow. Where is that thing? I can't see it," Kari said.

The smell of rotten eggs drifted into my nostrils. "Ick! What is that terrible smell?" I cried. I could feel a blast of warm, wet breath, and the smell made me gag. I stumbled backward and something that felt like a claw jammed into my rib cage. I let out a muffled cry and spun around.

It was a broom handle. I grabbed it. Now I was ready for the monster. I had a weapon. It would not take me easily. The shadow grew and dropped into a crouch, ready to pounce.

A blast of hot air hit us and a horrible roar blasted our ears. I still couldn't see it, but I knew it was ready to attack. Then the shadow leaped into the air.

We all jumped back about two feet. I aimed my broom and prepared to battle the two-headed beast. My friends were quickly digging in the junk around us for weapons.

Where did the monster land? I felt its breath and heard it sucking in air. I could hear it. I could feel it. I could smell it, but I could not see it.

Juan jumped in front of us and went into a karate stance. He yelled, "Monster, I want you to know that these hands are registered with the police as dangerous weapons."

Matthew laughed at him. "Juan, that is the oldest, cheapest movie line there is. That line always means you don't know anything at all about karate."

"Listen, Mr. Know-It-All, do you think a two-headed monster is going to spend its days watching old movies? For all it knows, I'm a master at karate, but now you've let the cat out of the bag," Juan answered angrily.

"We don't have time to fight each other. We need to conquer this thing and get out of here," I told them as I pushed my broom handle between them.

"She's right, Juan. Just cut out the movie stuff, and let's find a way out of here," Matthew spit out.

The beast roared loudly again. It was closer. It sounded like it was over our heads. I looked into the supports of the basement ceiling. I saw nothing. It roared again.

Kari jumped back and fell over something. She landed in a stack of boxes. As she struggled to her feet, I saw her grab something on the wall. She gave out a yell.

"What is it?" I asked her.

"I can't believe it, but I think I've found a door handle. That should mean there's a door behind these boxes," she yelled at us.

Matthew and Juan picked up the boxes and tossed them toward where we thought the monster was. I stood guard with my broom. If I couldn't smack the beast, I would at least sweep up the basement.

"It *is* a door!" Juan yelled excitedly.

"What if there is another monster on the other side?" Matthew cautiously asked.

Kari turned to him and said, "Don't be so pessimistic. I'm going to open it."

She pulled the door open, and I bolted through it with her. Seconds behind us, Matthew and Juan dove through and pulled the door shut. It was terribly dark in the room.

"I can't see a thing," I said.

Kari interrupted me. "Juan, stop that!"

"Stop what?"

"That heavy breathing. You're always trying to scare us. This place does a good enough job of that," Kari answered.

"I'm not doing anything," he said.

"Maybe it's coming from over there," Matthew told us. He wanted to direct us, but we couldn't see his hand. I stared around the dark room. Then I saw what Matthew was talking about. Two yellow eyes stared at us. They were large and blinked in time with the breathing.

"What do we do now?" I asked in a whisper.

"We have two choices. We could stay in this room and get eaten by a beast with yellow eyes, or we could go back into the other room and become dinner for a two-headed monster. I don't think that I like either option," Matthew said.

The eyes grew larger. The monster in the dark room was coming closer. I took a few steps back, but I couldn't see where I was going. I stumbled. I crashed against something hard and sharp with an angled corner. Could it be? I let out the loudest yell I could make.

"I found some stairs!" I hollered.

"Where do they go?" Matthew asked.

"What difference does it make?" I snapped at him.

"Each time we make a move it gets worse," he answered.

"Listen, it's dark. There's a creature about a foot away from us, and we have a set of stairs that lead somewhere. I can see light up there at the bottom of a door. That alone is enough for me," I insisted.

"I'm gone, dudes," Juan yelled as he pushed his way past me and up the steps. Kari came by me next, and I fell in behind her. Matthew followed us. It was hard to see in the dark, and we kept slipping and tripping on the steps. I heard Matthew tumble.

"Any broken bones?" Kari asked when he landed at the bottom of the stairs.

Matthew just groaned.

Kari called to Juan, "Get the door open. We'll help Matthew."

Kari and I ran down the stairs until we bumped into Matthew. The yellow eyes seemed just inches away from him. We felt around and found Matthew's arms.

Kari yelled, "Yank him up. We've got to get out of here."

Suddenly, the monster roared. It was next to my ear. I pulled on Matthew's arm, and we flew up the steps in a few seconds.

Matthew was mumbling, "*It Came from Beneath the Basement*." I wasn't sure what it meant, but at that point I wasn't about to stop and ask him.

The yellow eyes followed us, but we added distance between us. We would be safe unless we couldn't get that door open.

"Open it, Juan!" Kari screamed. It wasn't a command; it was more like she was pleading.

The door popped open and the steps were bathed in light. I didn't even take a second to turn around and look at the monster behind me. Instead, I pushed Matthew through the door and followed him into what appeared to be a kitchen. There was one small light bulb on over the sink. After all the darkness we had been through, it was like a lighthouse beam.

Juan slammed the door shut with a loud bang. We threw our backs against the wood, and I was the first to blow out a sigh of relief. Then I asked

Matthew what he had meant by "it came from beneath the basement."

We slid down the door and sat on the floor as Matthew responded, "That's the name of a *Tales of Terror* episode. These kids get locked in a basement with a couple of monsters."

Once again, our adventures seemed to be lifted from a TV show. I was still trying to decide whether our monsters were real when something whistled through the air above us and pierced the wooden door.

The four of us looked up at the same time. Kari screamed, "It's a butcher knife. Hide!"

There weren't many places to go. In fact, there was no place to hide. Juan's quick thinking saved our lives. He sprang toward the kitchen table and gripped the corner to pull it over. The top crashed against the hardwood flooring. We followed his lead and scooted behind the protection of the table.

I said with surprise, "Juan, that was really cool. What made you think of it?"

"I read it in a book about two kids who get attacked by their own house," he answered.

"I've got to start reading more of those books. That book might have saved our lives," Kari told us while she giggled. "By the way, did anyone see who threw the knife at us?"

"Nope." We all answered. Then we sat and listened.

There was no sound. There was no movement. Finally, Matthew said, "Is it safe?"

Juan rolled to the edge of the table and peeked around it. He turned back to us with a huge smile and said, "You will never guess what's on the other side of this table."

I peered over the upturned table. I expected to see some kind of monster. Instead I saw a very sweet-looking old woman. She was no taller than we were, but quite a bit plumper. Her gray hair was pulled back and rolled into a ball on the back of her head. Thin wire-rimmed glasses sat low on her nose. She was gazing over them in our direction.

I turned back to the others and joyfully said, "There's a very nice-looking grandmother standing in the kitchen smiling at us. I think it's safe. She looks like a picture I once saw of my great-grandmother." I stuck my head out from behind the table and said, "Hi."

She began talking to me, "I'm really sorry about that. I keep asking my boys not to play pranks on people when they visit."

"So, none of what we saw was real? It was just your kids playing jokes on us, ma'am?" Kari asked. She turned to us and said, "It's just what we thought."

The old woman nodded vaguely. "Please, call me Mother," she said. "Can I make you something to eat? I'm a very good cook."

"Sure, that would be great. Could you also show us how we can get out of here?" Juan asked.

"So many people have come in here and asked that question. It is so lonely around here. Even the master of the house has been very quiet. He and his dinner party have been sitting there for so long," Mother told us.

We looked at each other. Didn't she know the dinner party had been over for years? The people around that table were not going to get up and go home.

Matthew said, "The front door is barred. Can you show us another way out of the house?"

"It seems that when children come to visit, they never come back. I love having children in the house. Now, let me get you all something to eat. I've got plenty of extras on the stove," Mother answered with a big grin stretching her wrinkles.

"Mother, you mentioned your children. Where are they now?" I probed.

"The boys are out digging in the yard. They have so many things to bury," she told us.

"Do you have any pictures of them?" I wanted more information. I needed to see what the boys looked like. They could have been the "monsters" we had run into. Nothing in this house surprised me anymore.

Mother walked toward a hallway. I didn't know

where it led, and I wasn't sure that I wanted to follow her. But she stopped and pointed to some photos on the wall.

"These are my boys," Mother said proudly.

I walked over to the pictures and stared at them. My three friends joined me out of curiosity. The three boys were dressed in Union soldier outfits from the Civil War.

Juan pointed at them and asked, "Did they get these pictures taken at a theme park? I had one done with my little brothers. We were dressed like cowboys."

Mother stared at him like she had no idea what he was talking about. Then I noticed why. Next to the photos was a letter from General Ulysses S. Grant saying how sad he was about the death of her three sons at Gettysburg.

Her three sons were ghosts.

"Mother," I said to her, "this letter from General Grant says that your sons died in the Civil War. That was a long time ago."

"Wasn't that nice of the good General to write me? They shipped the boys back here, and I had them buried in the backyard. The three little trouble-makers have been inviting friends over to join them for years. Isn't it sweet of them to share their eternal resting place with so many of the town's citizens?" she told us through her beaming smile.

Kari caught on to what I was doing. We needed all the information we could get to figure out what was happening and how to get out of the house. I thought these crazy things were all part of the screen test. Yet I didn't think the TV studio would try to scare us away. And if no one was trying to scare us, maybe this was all real. *Father in heaven*, I prayed. *We don't know exactly what we're facing but with your help I know we'll get through it.*

Kari asked, "Mother, what can you tell us about the house?"

"Oh, this house has many tales. If it could talk, you would never believe them," she answered in a very serious and somber tone.

"We would love to hear some," I said. Matthew and Juan did not understand, but they were at least willing to humor her and us.

"Well, there was the time that the nice man in the gray pinstripe suit came to visit," she said.

"I think that we saw that suit a little earlier," Matthew edged in.

"Don't tell me he's up to those old tricks again. If I have told him once, I have told him a thousand times, 'Don't scare the children.' He thinks it's so funny to jump out of closets and walk around in the dark. He is quite harmless. The next time you see him, pay him no mind at all," she encouraged us.

"Maybe you should send him out to be dry cleaned," Juan cracked. Then he got serious. "When we were in the basement, we saw some animals. Can you tell me about them?" Juan said.

"Pets. They are my boys' pets. Those kids bring home the strangest-looking things. But they always did bring home every stray animal. Children, that is enough about my house. Wouldn't you all like something to eat? Let me fix you a few plates of good old-fashioned home cooking. What do you say, kids?" Mother asked with great enthusiasm.

As we followed her back to the kitchen, I quietly said to the others, "Do you all realize that if her sons died in the Civil War then she is either the oldest person on earth, or not of this earth?"

Juan joined in, "I vote for the second option. She is the most bizarre person I ever met except for old Mr. Rose, the math teacher. That guy is really weird, a math wacko extraordinaire."

"Juan, I really don't care about math class or anything at school. I just want out of here," Matthew told him. He dropped his voice to a whisper. "When she gets to the stove, I'm going to check out the back door. It looks open."

"Do you remember where the back door goes?" I asked.

"Yeah, back to the graveyard. But we survived it once and I'm sure that we can do it again," he told us.

Mother grabbed some plates from the cupboard and put them on the table after Kari and I set it back up on its legs. She moved back to the stove and picked up a big pan of something. She carried it with great care over to the table and set it right in the middle. It smelled terrible. I hoped it tasted better.

"This is so good. It's my boys' favorite. They go hunting and bring it back, and I cook it up. I have to warn you though, the boys love this stuff, and they

99

will fight for it. I've seen them pull out swords to see who would get the last bowl. If they show up, get out of their way," she laughed as she said it.

"Let's try it. I'm hungry," Juan said with joy.

Matthew edged to the back door to see if we could escape. Mother was not watching. She was busy grinning at the pot of food. I wanted to see what was inside. Mother's fingers wrapped around the little handle on the lid. She lifted it off.

Kari's hand went to her mouth to keep her from barfing. Juan pushed himself away from the table and jumped up, while I gagged.

The pot was filled with guts. It was the kind of stuff you see in horror movies. I was afraid to open my mouth in case more than words came out.

I concentrated on breathing in and out slowly to calm my stomach down. The sound of feet stomping on the back porch distracted me. Was it the sons? In another moment my fear was realized when I heard a voice call from the back porch, "Mother, I hope you have dinner ready. You have three hungry sons at your back door."

"Run for it!" Matthew yelled. I was the first one out of the kitchen, but I did not know which way to go. I headed down the hallway where the photos were.

The hall ended at the living room and just beyond that was the foyer. There was a light on in the living room that gave the foyer a dim gray look. It was an improvement over a dark black room.

I could see that the front door to the house was no longer barred. As I ran, I prayed, *Thank you, Father, for giving us a way out. At least I think it is. If it isn't, then I need to trust that you'll protect us.*

"Keep running," I yelled. "The front door is no longer blocked." We hit the foyer's slippery marble floor and skidded to a stop in front of the door. My hand shot out toward the knob. Before I could grab it, Kari knocked my hand away and pointed to a note nailed to the door.

Matthew ripped the note off and opened it. It read, "If you want to pass the screen test go to the recreation room on the other side of the living room."

Juan cheered. "See, it wasn't that bad. Let's get to the rec room and sign the contract to become the next hosts of *Tales of Terror.* This is going to be great."

Matthew slowed him down and pointed out, "Juan, it doesn't say that we've passed the test. It only says to go to the rec room if we want to pass the test."

"That's the same thing," Juan argued.

"No, it isn't," I added to the argument.

"I guess the only way to find out is to go to the rec room and see what's there," Juan challenged.

We were a little more cautious as we walked back through the living room and into another hallway. It was longer, and I felt like we were heading to the back of the haunted mansion. The hallway got darker as we went farther. It came to an abrupt stop in front of a large set of double doors.

"I guess this is when we find out if we're the hosts, or if we still have more screen test to go," Matthew said.

"Let's go in and see who is right," Juan suggested.

He opened the door. It was dimly lit, but what a room it was. It had a Ping-Pong table, a pool table, three pinball machines, and a large screen TV with popcorn and cans of cola sitting in front of it.

"This is fantastic," Matthew said. "I have to admit that Juan was right. We must have passed the test. I guess we're supposed to chill here until someone comes to meet us."

Kari and I jumped over the back of the big, over-stuffed couch in front of the TV. I snapped open a canned drink and took a small swig. I didn't even trust America's favorite cola in this place. It tasted good, so I downed the rest of it in a couple of gulps. I had not realized how thirsty I could get when I'm being scared to death.

"This is some setup. It must be where we hang out whenever we're not on the air. I could get to like this," Kari said to me. We both laughed, and I leaned back on the couch, picking up the remote control. I pushed the button, and the TV came on.

It was a fitting show. It was about kids being chased through a haunted house. Pretty typical stuff and not very scary after you have actually experienced it.

Matthew and Juan sat next to us on the couch. Juan leaned forward, grabbed a cola, and said, "I'm trying to think about what I'm going to say to all the kids at school."

"Tell them the truth. We are the most awesome set of hosts that *Tales of Terror* will ever have," Kari responded.

"I guess that will do," he said, and then laughed.

Matthew sucked in a breath and let it out slowly. "I was just thinking."

"Wow, you thought twice in one night. This ought to be in the *Guinness Book of World Records*," Juan joked. I could tell he was relaxing. Juan and Matthew always joked around when they were just hanging out.

"Real funny. Not!" Matthew tossed back. "I was wondering, what if the monsters and all the other stuff had been real instead of fake? What would we do?"

"We could draw on the spiritual warfare stuff in the Bible. Pastor Goodman mentioned it last Sunday in his message," Kari said thoughtfully.

"I think you're onto something here," I told her.

Kari continued, "In the Book of Ephesians, it tells us that we don't wrestle against real people when it comes to spiritual things. We wrestle against unseen beings from the devil's army."

"I remember that section. My question is, what are we supposed to do?" Matthew asked.

"Pastor Goodman said we need to put on spiritual armor," Kari answered.

I was confused. "How do we get spiritual armor? I must have missed that part."

"He plans to talk about that part next Sunday," Kari answered.

"Then I'm there even if I have to walk," Matthew told us.

"I'm coming with you," Juan added. He settled onto the couch. "Does anyone know what's going on in this movie?"

"The last I noticed, four kids were being chased through a haunted house. When we started talking, I lost track of the plot," I replied.

"It must be an upcoming episode of *Tales of Terror* because the four kids are sitting in this room. Look, behind them is a monster. That is such an old trick. Why couldn't they come up with something a little more original than a monster sneaking up on unsuspecting kids? That never really happens," Juan griped.

"Actually the plot isn't from a new episode. It looks a lot like the movie *Don't Open the Door*. But that movie was in black and white. This must be a remake of it," Matthew told us.

"I'll bet it's going to be the first episode we host. We better watch it—think of it as homework," Juan said with a laugh.

We sat watching the four kids on the TV. The camera angle made it difficult to see what they looked like. One thing was very strange. The kids in the movie were dressed exactly like we were. The monster on the TV kept inching its way closer to the characters. They sat with their backs to the slimy creature. They didn't even know it was sneaking up behind them.

"This is stupid. Monsters just don't sneak up on people," Matthew said, and he leaned forward to get his cola. I noticed that one of the kids on TV leaned forward at the same time. So I tried it. I leaned forward. The kid on the TV did too.

"I've got some very disturbing news. Those four kids are us. There must be a camera on us," I told them. I tried not to show my panic.

"That's crazy," Kari said. "If that was us on TV, there would be a monster behind us." We all turned around together. There behind us, inches from taking a bite out of Kari's head, was the monster from the TV.

"Ahhhhhh!" we screamed in unison.

Matthew was holding a bowl of popcorn. He flung it
at the monster smacking it right on the nose. It
reared back and moved a few feet away. The rest of
us got the idea and began to throw whatever we
could find. Cola cans went hurtling through the air,
bouncing off the head, nose, and arms of the roaring
slimy creature.

"There is only one way out of here, and that slime
ball's standing between us and the door. What do
we do?" Matthew asked.

"We have got to get him to move away from the
door," I answered.

"Sure, maybe we can just throw an arm over there
for him to chase and chew on. Do you have any
extra?" Juan responded sarcastically.

The monster crawled toward us again. Kari and I
leaped off the couch and onto the table in front of us.
As we jumped to the floor, the table twisted. I realized
it was actually the projecting camera of the TV. It was

one of the original big-screen projection TVs. We'd had one in our house before we moved to Grove City.

Matthew jumped on it next, and the table turned some more. When Juan jumped, it spun around until the light was directly in the monster's eyes.

When the colored beams hit the beast and projected our images onto him, he backed away. It gave me an idea.

"The light is too bright. If we can back him into the corner using the projection table, then we can slip out the door and get away," I told the others.

"Sounds like a plan to me," Kari agreed.

Matthew and Juan did not even wait to nod their heads. They both grabbed the table and started to twist it and drag it toward the door. When the colorful beams of light struck the monster, it retreated. Juan kept pushing the table toward the door while Matthew kept it aimed.

Kari and I carefully stayed hidden with them behind the lights until we were close to the door. Kari jumped from the beam's protection and bolted toward the opening. But she moved too early. The monster shifted its slimy, beady-eyed face and blocked the light with its hand. When the beast saw her, it moved her way.

It lunged and missed her, but slammed the partially open door. Kari raced back to the protection of the projection table. She said, "I'm sorry. I got scared and tried to run too soon. What do we do now?"

Matthew looked at her, "Don't worry about it. We're all scared. The best thing we can do is to stay together." Matthew turned to Juan. "Let's try it again. We'll get the projector next to the door so that thing has to go through the beam to get us."

The two carefully worked the TV's projector closer to the door. Then Kari opened the door again. The monster roared and swung with its gigantic, sharp-nailed, green hand but couldn't reach us. We slipped through the door.

The hallway led to the living room and the kitchen. We knew we didn't want to go to the kitchen. That was certain trouble with Mother's three sons chowing down on the leftovers from whatever it was they buried. I did not want to go from the rec room into the frying pan or, especially, into Mother's pot.

Kari must have been thinking the same thing. She turned at the entrance to the living room and came to a stop. She was winded from the sprint down the hallway. We pulled up behind her.

"What now?" Matthew asked.

"Should we try the front door again?" I asked.

"Do we have many other choices? Let's go for it!" Juan yelled.

We started toward the archway that led to the foyer when a figure stepped into the frame. I could not make out who or what it was at first. I stopped along with the others. We huddled together.

"Who are you?" Juan asked softly.

"Hello, kids. I am so glad you came back. Are you ready for a little something to eat now?"

Mother!

I turned around. Down one hallway was a slimy monster. In the kitchen were three Civil War soldiers
munching down on guts. In front of us was a sweet
little old lady who wanted to cook us for dinner. If we
could get around her to the front door, we could
possibly escape. If we couldn't . . .

"The front door doesn't have bars on it anymore.
I bet we could get out of it," Juan whispered.

"How do we get around Mother?" Matthew whispered back.

"I've got an idea," I said quietly. "Watch this and
come to my rescue if I yell for help."

I started walking in Mother's direction. My three
friends looked at me like I had gone a little crazy. I
made myself grin as I said, "Mother, I am so glad
you're still here. We felt so bad about having to rush
out on you, but you know how teenagers are. I think
we would love to have some dinner now. Is there
someplace we could wash our hands?"

She grinned and answered, "Of course there is. The door at the top of the stairs is a washroom. While you're doing that, I'll go heat up some more of my boys' favorite meal."

"That is a wonderful idea, Mother. By the way, what do you call that special meal? Could I possibly get the recipe for my mom?" I requested. The smile I stretched across my face was so big it hurt.

Mother seemed proud and delighted that someone appreciated her food. "Sure, little girl, I will get the recipe. It is simple to make, but I don't really have a name for it. I just call it the boys' favorite. I'll even wrap some up for your mom to try." The old woman turned and left the doorway.

"That was brilliant, Bethany," Matthew said. "You should try out for the Christmas play at church."

"I want to get out of this haunted house before I make any future plans. Someone check the front door," I directed.

Kari pulled it open. I expected to go dashing out and down the street to my own warm little house. But behind the door was a wall of disappointment. A brick wall, in fact. The front door was no longer an exit, and the back door was blocked by the Brothers Ghoul, waiting to tell us some very grim stories about our future.

Kari looked at us and asked, "What now?"

None of us had time to answer. We heard Mother

say, "Would one of you boys go get those nice kids so we can have them for dinner?"

We gulped. It was obvious that we were next in line for the pot of gut stew. Without even talking we all bolted up the staircase. When we reached the top, Juan stated, "We need to search every room and find an open window that we can use for our escape."

"I suggest we split up," said Kari.

"Forget it. We are staying together," I said very firmly. The others agreed, so we crept down the hallway to the first door on our left. I stood by it and warned the others, "We need to be quiet in case there is something inside that we don't want to see. Let's not give it any advance warning."

Juan answered, "Okay." But he forgot to whisper.

Unfortunately, I had already opened the door to the dark room. The hall light, which was on, cast a dim light into the room. I entered the room and looked around. The windows were covered by heavy curtains. Kari walked over to them and pushed them aside. We saw more bricks.

Then I noticed something and quietly asked, "What is that big black thing on the other side of the room?" The bedroom was very large and shadowy.

"It must be the bed. I don't see anything else big enough to be a bed in here," Matthew answered. "I'm going closer to take a look."

Matthew tiptoed to the middle of the room and

came to a dead stop. He turned back to us with wide eyes. Somehow, he spit out the phrase, "It's a coffin."

He said it too loudly. I could see a dark form sitting up in the coffin. It flapped a big black cape in the air.

"It's a vampire!" I screamed.

Kari dashed back from the window. Juan pulled the door wide open for a quick exit, and Matthew wasted no time in joining them. I stood frozen in my tracks until six hands grabbed me from behind and yanked me into the hall.

We all ran down the hall. None of us knew where we were going, but we knew what we were running from. The hallway was long. The farther we went, the darker it got.

Kari is the school's fastest runner. She was at least three feet ahead of us. Then she deliberately cut to her left. Crashing into a doorway brought her to an abrupt and painful stop.

We tried to stop fast, but smacked into Kari and shoved her another three feet down the hall. When I looked up at her, I saw why Kari had stopped so quickly.

The vampire was standing at the end of the hall. "How did he get there?" I asked.

"I'm not waiting around to ask him about his Olympic running techniques. Let's get out of here," Juan yelled.

We turned around to run away from the vampire. Standing sweetly beneath the one light in the hall was Mother grinning her All-American Grandmother grin. "Did you forget that we were having you for dinner? My boys are waiting, and they are starving. Maybe one of you could give me a hand. That ought to hold them until you're cooked and properly seasoned."

"Middle schooler stew—that can't be good for anyone. Especially for us," I said.

"I feel like I did this backward and I've just gone from the fire into the frying pan. Any suggestions?" Matthew asked.

"Yeah, follow me," Juan commanded. He shoved the door that we were standing next to open. None of us questioned what was behind it. We jumped inside and slammed it behind us.

"I think we're back in the fire again," Juan said.

I looked up and in the faint light coming from under the door, I saw a set of stairs that probably went to the attic. I turned to the others and said, "We have to climb those stairs and find a way out of here."

The sound of Mother knocking at the door sent us racing up the steps. Matthew was the first one through the attic door. Then Kari, Juan, and I came tumbling in behind him. Kari pulled the door shut.

We had gone back into complete darkness. I called to the others, "Where is everyone?"

Kari touched my arm and said, "I'm next to you, and Juan is next to me."

"Help me! I've been slimed!" Matthew's voice sounded muffled.

"Matthew, where are you?" I gasped.

"Hey, I just found something that will help us," Kari said. She had backed into the wall and felt something poke her. When she reached to see what it was, she discovered a light switch.

Kari flipped on the switch and a bare light bulb went on above us. The attic was filled with old junk and trunks. It looked like a great place to explore— if it were your grandmother's. But here I wasn't too interested in exploring.

"There's Matthew," Juan yelled.

Matthew had been hung by his shirt on a coat hook. His body was coated with a greenish slime that dripped from him onto the bare wood floor. It looked like the same stuff that covered our monster friend in the rec room.

He smiled at us and said, "As you can see I got a little hung up."

I could feel the laughter deep inside me, and then

it broke out like a volcano. Kari started laughing, too, and Juan was on the floor trying to hold back his loud honking laugh.

"I'm glad I can amuse you all. Could you get me down?" Matthew pleaded.

"What? And touch all that slime?" Kari said.

"You're right, Kari. He's far too messy. Maybe we should leave him there to dry," I suggested.

"Ha, ha, ha," Matthew mocked us.

Juan and I pulled him down off the hook while Kari roamed around the attic. She threw an old rag at Matthew to clean himself off with.

He wiped his face and arms while he described how something had grabbed him. He was hung on the hook, and then he was squirted with slime.

"I'm glad it slimed you, Matthew," Kari said.

"Nice friend you are," he retorted.

"If the slime monster got in and out, then we can too. Fortunately for us, the slime monster stepped in the goo. We can follow its escape route," Kari stated as she pointed to the floor.

The slime led us to one of the side walls. In the wall was a panel on hinges. Kari pushed it, and it moved freely. I looked inside and there was a bit of slime within.

"It looks to me like we have another secret passageway. Who would like to do the honors on this one?" I asked.

Juan slid into the hole first without saying a word. I was surprised at how brave we were becoming—or foolish. Matthew volunteered to go next. I followed him. I was praying for our safety as I crossed through the wall panel.

Inside, the wall was dark. "Kari, it's your turn," I called back to her as I swung the panel open to let in some light.

"I'll be there in a second. I've got something I need to do," she answered.

I held the panel open and saw her cross the attic to the door. I thought she was going to lock it, but instead she turned out the light. The attic went dark.

"Kari, what are you doing?" I called to her. Suddenly the floor to the secret passage gave way, and we went sliding. This was getting old. This time we didn't slide far before we were gently curved into a sitting position and then deposited in a long, narrow passageway that was lit.

"Kari did not make it," I said. "She went back to turn off the light when the floor opened up on us. I think we should go back to get her."

Matthew looked very seriously at me, "Bethany, we're stuck here. We have to get out of our predicament before we can go back up and help her."

"The best thing we can do is to keep our cool and find the way out," Juan added. "Let's look along this passage. But be careful. It looks more like a bridge than a hallway."

We started our walk along it. To our right was a wall. On our left was thick glass. I was glad it was thick because beyond it were a variety of caged monsters. Some had two heads. Some had no head. One of them had the head of a horse and the body of a monkey.

"What is this place?" I asked.

"It must be the zoo for the Munsters," Juan cracked.

"Nope," Matthew said. "This is a scene from *Dr. Shocker's Laboratory*. And what happened to me in the attic also happened to that comedian, Steve Markum, in the comedy horror movie he made. But there's something I don't understand."

"What?" Juan asked.

"If these are all scenes from movies then why do they seem so real? Why do I feel like I'm in danger?" Matthew said. None of us could answer his question, but it made me think. I knew we were getting close to finding out what was real and what was just an illusion.

We said very little as we walked to the end of the passage. Each cell we passed had a more bizarre monster creeping and dwelling in it. I could not wait to get out of this place and find Kari. I was worried about her, but I knew I could trust in God. He is everywhere, and he could take care of her and us at the same time in different places.

Juan led our single file line. He stopped and

Matthew and I stopped behind him. He turned around and said, "It's a door. Do we go through it? Dr. Shocker could be on the other side."

"We have to get back to Kari. I vote we go ahead," I stated.

Matthew was a little more practical. "We have no choice. This is the only way out."

Juan pushed the door open, and we found ourselves in one of the upstairs bedrooms of the haunted house. The door slowly shut behind us.

In the dark room we heard, "Hello, children." Mother and her three boys were waiting for us.

We all screamed as Mother flipped on the light and her three sons moved our way. The four looked so ghostly. They hadn't appeared like that in the kitchen.

Mother spoke to us, "Children, you have been very naughty. Mother wanted to have you for dinner, and you ran away. And you woke up the guests in the house. You disappointed my sons. They wanted to play football with you."

One of the Brothers Ghoul spoke, "Yeah, we like football." He then pulled a foot from behind his back and threw it to one of the other brothers.

Matthew and Juan moved close to me when I let out a quiet, "Yuck." This time we were in big trouble. The doorway out was to our left, and one of the boys headed that way. They were not about to let us go again.

"Where is your other little girlfriend?" Mother asked. "Has she left?"

I whispered to Matthew, "That's a good sign. It means they don't have Kari."

He answered back. "A lot of good that will do us. Maybe she can speak at our funerals and tell everyone that we were good to the last bite."

Juan added, "That is if she hasn't been caught by the vampire or the Slime Monster or that fancy suit of clothes."

"Thanks, guys, you really brightened my day and gave me a boost of encouragement. I'll make sure to turn your names in for the school's Booster Club," I shot at them. I didn't need to hear more depressing thoughts. We needed to focus on finding a way out.

Brother Ghoul One circled us from the left. Brother Ghoul Two went to the right, and the third one walked slowly toward us with Mother next to him. He was the one who spoke before, and he opened his mouth again.

"You kids messed up our little playground out back. You bothered our pets in the basement. You interrupted the dinner party in the dining room and woke up the Count. You have been very bad," he said in an eerie voice.

Mother started talking while she shook her finger at us. "Usually we don't let people leave when they visit, but the boys said that none of you have enough meat on you. Do you promise to leave this place and never come back for any reason?"

I was the first one to agree, "Yes, we'll go, and we will stay away and never bother you again." I could not believe that we were going to be let go.

As I looked at Mother and her sons, I was sure I saw them fade out and then fade back in. Then they looked snowy like on a television when the channel doesn't come in well.

It got stranger. The four walked backward saying things we couldn't understand. Then Mother and the boys were back to their own ghostly selves. Mother began talking again. She was shaking her finger just as before.

She said, "Usually we don't let people leave when they visit but the boys said that none of you have enough meat on you. Do you promise to leave this place and never come back for any reason?"

It was the exact phrase she used before. This confused me, but I answered again, "Mother, as I said a minute ago we agree to never come back."

Mother and her sons faded in and out again. They turned snowy and moved backward. Mother shook her finger at us again while she said, "Usually we don't let-buzz-leave-buzz-when they-buzz-visit but the-buzz-said that-buzz-of you have enough-buzz-on you. Do you-buzz-to leave this-buzz-and never-buzz-buzz-buzz-come back for any-buzz?"

Juan looked at us and at them. He scratched his head and asked, "What is going on here?"

We did not have to wait long for the answer. The door behind us flew open. I could not believe who was standing there with a crowbar tightly gripped in her hand.

"Kari!" I yelled.

She walked toward us holding the hard piece of metal. She looked very angry. "I will show you what is going on."

Juan, Matthew, and I backed away from her. The monsters, ghosts, and ghouls of the house must have taken over her mind. Kari walked right by us and then passed right through the ghostly figures of Mother and one of her sons. I was sure they were going to grab her, but instead Mother faded in and out, retraced her steps and started the same speech over again.

"Usually we don't let-buzz-buzz-buzz-when-buzz-buzz-visit-buzz-said-buzz-of-buzz-buzz-buzz-buzz-on you. Do you-buzz-buzz-buzz-buzz-buzz-and never-buzz-buzz-buzz-come-buzz-buzz-any-buzz?"

Not only were her words breaking up, but so was her image. Kari continued over to the wall and inserted the crowbar into the edge of a wooden panel on the wall. She popped it open quietly.

Inside was a control room that was bigger than the one at the studio where we took our first screen test. I expected to see Mr. Christensen and the cameraman, Rick, behind the controls. Instead, four middle schoolers sat in the chairs. They were pushing buttons frantically and didn't even notice we were watching.

One of them yelled at the others, "What's wrong? We almost had them ready to drop out."

A girl with dark curly hair responded, "I don't know. It's like we've lost control over the three dimensional projections."

Another girl stood up. She was dressed just like Mother, but without Mother's face. "It looks like I'll have to do this one live. Where's my mask?"

The first boy said, "I thought I knew everything about computers, but this is something I've never seen before. It's like the computer images have a life of their own. I wish I knew what was causing it."

"I'm causing it," Kari said. In her hand was a large remote control that obviously ran all the equipment.

"Who are they? What's going on here?" Matthew questioned.

I looked at the middle schoolers in the booth. They all looked a little guilty.

"This is the team in competition with us to be the hosts for *Tales of Terror*," Kari explained.

"Kari, why didn't you follow us?" I quizzed her.

"When we were in the attic, I noticed a reflection of light coming off a camera lens. I knew that there was something more real than unreal behind all this. I turned out the light. I knew they would follow you three and not me. Then I sneaked down to the basement to get this crowbar I'd seen there. I needed it to pry back the wood paneling," she answered.

Juan looked at the other team. "Why did you do this to us?"

The girl dressed like Mother lowered her head in embarrassment and answered, "We wanted to be the hosts. We figured if we scared you four off, the job was ours. We did our second screen test yesterday, and Mr. Christensen showed us how all this stuff worked. Since we're all computer wizards, we learned how to use the special effects quickly. We slipped in and called you to come for your screen test. I'm sorry, it was a really stupid idea to try to scare you away."

The curly-haired girl added, "We never expected you to last this long. In fact, we never dreamed you'd ever come inside the house. We thought the graveyard scene would be enough to send you running away."

"I've gotta admit," said one of the boys, "I'd like to know what it is about you that helps you to be so brave.

Juan answered, "Let's just say that *God* is brave

enough for all four of us." Then he looked at Matthew, Kari, and me and asked with a smile, "How many times are we supposed to forgive?"

In unison we answered, "Seventy times seven, Jesus said."

Our team and theirs shook hands.

The next evening we had our real screen test. We handled each event gracefully, with just enough fright to look good for the cameras. Our opponents had gone to Mr. Christensen at the TV studio and confessed what they had done.

After our screen test he got the four of us together at the Big and Beefy Burger Buddies. He said as we ate, "I must tell you that I was impressed with both groups. You handled yourselves great during the screen test.

"I also watched the video from your first night at the house. I have never seen such perseverance from a group of middle schoolers. You hung in there, no matter what happened to you. What you saw is the latest in technology, which all looked pretty real in the soft lighting. I am going to suggest that the studio hire all eight of you and let you alternate weeks as hosts."

We all looked surprised. It seemed like he was rewarding the other group for its deceptive acts. But

Mr. Christensen's next remarks cleared things up. "That is, after our computer wizards spend a few weeks cleaning up around the 'haunted' house."

"Even the cemetery?" Juan asked.

"Yes, especially the cemetery," Mr. Christensen answered with a laugh.

Matthew had been right. All the scenes we experienced came from movies that were on *Tales of Terror*. And I had been right. I could trust God no matter what happened to us. We all learned that what seems unreal usually has a real explanation.

The kids moved slowly through the old school. It was dark, and all they could hear was dripping water. Suddenly, from behind them came a snarling, angry werewolf.

As the werewolf leaped into the air, the camera faded on the movie scene and cut to the four of us. It was our first night to host the show. Matthew was enjoying and overplaying his role.

His face was covered in green slime. He leaned forward in his seat and said, "Don't let next week's episode slip away from you. Tune in for 'Werewolves Make Great Pets' and join our co-hosts for a frighteningly good time. Ha, ha, ha." His laugh was very scary sounding.

The camera faded, and we were done. I looked at the others and said, "You know something? This isn't as much fun as I thought it would be. I guess after you've lived through a night filled with real terror, the movie stuff is not as exciting."

"I was hoping someone would say that," Juan spoke up with the grin of his that always said we were going on an adventure. He continued, "I was reading in the newspaper about this warehouse down by the river. Strange things have been happening there. I thought maybe we could go down there and check it out."

Matthew shook his head no. I wasn't too sure about the idea, but Kari raised her fist in the air and said, "Yes! When do we go?"

If I didn't like these people so much, I'd find a safer set of friends. But how many kids that love a good mystery could I find in a town like Grove City?

Read and collect all of
Fred E. Katz's

SpineChillers™
Mysteries

*Turn the page
for a spine-chilling preview . . .*

Hospitals Make Me Sick

Book #11
by Fred E. Katz

While on a trip in the mountains with his brother Michael and their cousin Deanna, Scotty injures his elbow and goes to a nearby hospital. To the trio's amazement, they soon learn that the hospital might be hazardous to their health. The chief doctors—Dr. Frankenstein and Dr. Jekyll— are quite spooky, the hospital gowns have bullseyes painted on them, and the only way to escape is to solve a mysterious riddle.

We screamed in unison.

"Children, this is a hospital. Please be quiet and stay in the appointed areas. Now, move along," said a very tall nurse with a pasty, gray skin. She looked like she could use a little sun.

I spoke quickly, "My brother cut his elbow. We're waiting for a doctor to patch him up."

As she ushered us down the hall, she said, "Well, you have come to the right place. We have quite a few doctors here. Let's see, Dr. Frankenstein is on the third floor. Dr. Jekyll is on the second, but I don't think Dr. Jekyll is right for you. He has a terrible bedside manner. Some patients even call him beastly. It's almost as if he becomes another person. . . . Dr. Frankenstein it is. He has had plenty of experience sewing up body parts. I'll take you there."

Deanna looked at me, then I looked at Scotty. I thought, *Was this lady just weird, or was she trying to be funny?* I was ready to make a run for it. I sized up Scotty; he could run if he had to. Then she led us through double doors into a dim hallway and to a round room. I could hear other people nearby. I felt better.

"Now, the three of you wait right here while I go get you a doctor. Hmm, I see that you don't have your hospital bracelet or patient's gowns. Three gowns and bracelets coming up," she said, then dashed into the hall.

I tried to explain that only my brother needed a doctor, but she didn't hear me. I turned to the others and whispered, "Is she the weirdest-looking thing you've ever seen?"

I was ready to leave, but the doctor walked in. He had on a white coat and rubber gloves. That seemed pretty normal. Then I noticed the blood splattered all over his coat and gloves.

"Now, what is the problem?" he asked.

Scotty lifted his arm. The doctor looked at it and said, "Looks like the right stuff was done to it already. I'll just check your reaction time."

He went to a big cabinet behind him and opened its doors. "I keep my reflex hammer in here some-where," he said. "No, that's not it," he mumbled as he moved aside a hypodermic needle three feet long. "Aha," he said as he whipped around holding a huge sledge hammer in the air. His eyes got glassy as a bizarre smile crossed his face.

He raised the hammer over his head. I jumped in front of my brother. "Could I see your license?" I asked with as much bravado as I could manage.

The doctor looked right at me and growled, "That would be unnecessary and unpleasant for you." He paused and added, "We don't need to check his re-actions. I should look at his throat. Let me get a tongue depressor."

The doctor dropped the sledge hammer back in the cabinet and then spun around holding a two-by-four that was about four feet long.

"This ought to do it," he said.

Scotty shut his mouth tight.

"All right, I'll give you a prescription and send you on your way," he said. "Then you'll be able to solve the riddle." He wrote something out and handed it to me.

I couldn't keep my mouth from dropping open when I read it. I passed it to Deanna, who passed it to Scotty. The prescription was for Fright Pills—"To be taken after every shriek."

Over the public address system we heard: "Veterinarian John Darby, please report to the front desk. The chain saw you ordered just arrived . . ."